Tongues of Flame

Tongues of Flame

TIM PARKS

GROVE PRESS, INC./NEW YORK

Published by Grove Press, Inc.
920 Broadway
New York, N.Y. 10010
First published in Great Britain in 1985 by William Heinemann, Ltd, London

Library of Congress Cataloging-in-Publication Data

Parks, Tim.
        Tongues of flame.

        I. Title.
PR6066.A6957T6   1986   823'.914   86-45239
ISBN 0-394-55299-7

Manufactured in the United States of America
First American Edition 1986

10 9 8 7 6 5 4 3 2

For Mark

The few half-remembered events of seventeen years ago which prompted me to write this novel have been altered beyond all recognition for the purposes of fiction. No reference to any living person is intended or should at any point be inferred.

T.P.

PART ONE

A Devil in the House

It was Donald Rolandson brought the Sword of the Spirit into our house and it would have been about 1968. The world was full of strange new things just then I remember; there were wars and threats of wars and marches, an explosion of new hairstyles and new religions, and so perhaps it wasn't surprising that the Sword of the Spirit should have arrived that year, the tongues of flame and the dove and all the things she brought with her like leaves in a whirlwind. Nevertheless, my mother wasn't pleased at first.

'I'm not sure quite who he thinks he is,' she said, 'or who he thinks he's going to impress, playing holier-than-thou.'

My father would have been peeling the shell off his boiled egg. He had a high opinion of Rolandson and anyway he never spoke at breakfast.

'If he wanted to play that game he could have joined the Quakers or the Plymouth Brethren,' Mother said, and she said, 'If he has to beat his breast in public I don't see why he has to go and do it here. And after the best kind of education like that too.'

She poured the tea.

'As if everything was all going to change suddenly, just because he'd arrived. But they all think that at first of course.'

And then she laughed. 'I suppose he'll grow out of it, bless his heart.'

She sat down with a grapefruit opposite Father and they looked at each other across the formica top of the table.

Father said, 'Where's Adrian?'

Mother turned to me. 'Go and get Adrian,' she said. 'Tell him to come down here at once. He'll be late for church.'

I went out of the kitchen and up the broad staircase. As soon as I was well out of the room they began to talk again, but I didn't hear what they said because the walls of our house were very thick and the doors likewise and anyway they both spoke very low.

My sister was in the study sitting on Father's desk, swinging her legs and speaking on the telephone to her boyfriend at the Missionary Training College in Croydon. I went up the stairs.

'Bugger,' Adrian said.

His room was quite dark with the curtains still drawn, the windows closed, and it smelt stale, of dirty socks and of sleep; the floor was littered with clothes and empty cups, record sleeves.

'That's what she said.'

'Groan,' he said. 'The hell with it. Say I've got a headache if you have to say something.'

Adrian hadn't been to church for more than six months now. In fact he didn't come down to breakfast very often either. But on Sunday Mother considered it a kind of duty, I think, to remind him this was the Lord's Day; and so it was she always sent me upstairs to wake him and to tell him he'd be late for church. She didn't go herself because she was afraid of Adrian. She was afraid she would hear him say something she didn't want to believe her son could say.

'They're loonies,' Adrian said. 'Bloody nuts.'

I went into my own room and put on my maroon tie and the herringbone jacket and combed my hair down to the collar, looking in the mirror.

In church Father preached about Gideon's men whom the Lord sorted out by making them drink water from a stream and the ones who picked up the water with their cupped hands so they could look over their shoulder while they drank, those ones He sent home because they didn't trust in Him completely but in their own eyes: but those who put their heads down and drank directly with their mouths, those ones He took to His bosom and He kept because they trusted in Him entirely. And my father said that in this world we shouldn't always be looking over our shoulders at new fashions and new ideas, nor even at our fiercest enemies, but that we should drink directly from the life-blood of Our Lord Jesus Christ who had given His Body for us.

In the stalls in his white surplice and blue Oxford hood, Rolandson said very loudly, 'Ay-men!'

'There he goes,' my mother whispered. 'He can't even keep quiet while his own vicar is preaching.'

'He wants to make a grand impression,' she said. 'You can see that a mile off.'

I always sat with my mother and we always put ourselves in the last pew of the church because my mother liked to be able to see exactly who was in the congregation and then also, in this position, she could make signs to my father to tell him whether his voice was carrying right to the back or not. If she lifted both hands and put them together over her mouth as if in concentration, then this was a sign that his voice wasn't carrying well and he had to speak up. But actually this was a favourite gesture of my mother's anyway, whenever she was trying to think quietly and seriously about something; and so sometimes, engrossed in the sermon, she would do it absent-mindedly and Father would start to boom with an enormous voice so that everybody in the congregation was taken by surprise and the younger people would turn round and grin at each other – 'the under-twenties', as my mother called them. But I roasted in embarrassment.

My sister, Anna, didn't sit with us at the back of the church; she sat in the front row right beneath the pulpit because after the sermon she would go up with two other girls and they would sing together with guitars on the white chancel steps. Anna was a great fan of Billy Graham's ever since she had seen him at a rally at Earls Court and she'd gone to the front to kneel before the Lord in the presence of thousands, even though she was already a Christian and had been for ages. So on the chancel steps she sang 'I Gotta Home in Gloryland that Outshines the Sun', and 'You Gotta Walk that Lonesome Valley', and all the other songs that were on the Billy Graham record, turn and turn about, one week after another.

When they finished singing 'What a Friend We have in Jesus', Rolandson said 'Ay-men' again in a loud, near ecstatic voice and some of the congregation said ay-men too because it was a sort of habit really to repeat what the clergymen said over these small things.

'I wouldn't mind,' my mother whispered to me, 'if he said "Ah-men", but why does he have to say "Ay-men, aaaay-men", as if we were at a blessed American Revivalist meeting or something?'

My father gave the blessing then, his favourite one: 'And now unto Him who is able to keep you without stumbling and without stain . . .' He used to make his voice rise and fall a little with the words so that it was mesmerizing – 'May the Lord bless you and keep you, yea, may the Lord cause his face even to shine upon you . . .'

And now, after the blessing, there was always a long moment of quiet which was supposed to be for silent prayer, and it was this moment, almost the end of it in fact when everybody was already half-ready to go, shuffling for gloves and hats and handbags, that Rolandson at last spoke out. He stood and spoke; and in the quiet and cold of the half-full church his voice was truly enormous.

'It is the Word of the Lord causes me to speak,' he boomed – the congregation froze still as one surprised animal – 'and the Sword of the Spirit opens this my mouth. Speak through me Holy Spirit: breathe on me Breath of God . . .' – and then he simply began to gabble very loud; to gabble, sounds quite indistinguishable as language or even words, but dramatic and rousing and guttural, and as he gabbled strangely like this he turned and slowly raised both arms towards the stained glass at the back of the church, through which the winter sun plunged on to bare pillars in great splashes of wine and blue. He went on like this for two or three whole minutes, gabbling, gabbling, gabbling; a noise of words without words. Then he stopped abruptly, but still held his arms raised, outstretched, draped with the white surplice like the pictures of the prophets in my Illustrated Revised Standard Version. The congregation began to fidget, ill at ease, and to lift their knees off their hassocks and wiggle their bottoms back on their pews. But my mother stayed still knelt, absolutely rigid with shock.

'It is the Lord hath spoken,' Rolandson finished with a

falling voice, 'and a great and mighty wind is blowing through our land. Let it touch even me, Lord, let it touch even me. Blessed be the Word of the Lord.'

He sank down to his knees and buried his head in his hands and appeared to weep.

★   ★   ★

At lunch we had lamb as always and there was Grandmother, my father's mother, who was deaf, and Anna's boyfriend, Ian, from the Missionary Training College in Croydon who always came on a huge Japanese motorbike. He had a small round freckled face with a broken nose and big ears and he grinned almost all the time, so that my father despised him, I think, though he never actually said anything. But if he hadn't despised him he would have said something to the contrary.

It was a very quiet lunch except that Grandmother wanted to complain about the water board who were digging up her front drive in Palmers Green and then Anna tried to start a conversation about the church in China, which was where Ian had been called to go as a missionary; but my parents wouldn't join in any of this. They didn't mention Rolandson either.

The cuckoo-clock squeaked out two as my father was scraping up the last of the cauliflower. We were late, which was serious Sundays with a sermon to prepare. He had to shout then to Grandmother to have her pass him the cruet, but she still didn't hear: she started talking about her drive again and whether the water board were going to have to pull up her rose-beds next; and so then Father lost his temper.

'Where's Adrian?' he demanded.

My mother said she didn't know, she hadn't seen the boy

6

for two or three days now: she made her lips puckered and grim in the open pale face she had.

'I'll tan that young laddie's hide so soon as I set eyes on him,' Father said. 'Skipping off all the time without so much as a by your leave to his family. It's offensive.' He didn't look up from his plate but ate rapidly and nervously, and he used to eat so close to his plate sometimes when he was in a mood, his glasses would steam up.

'Where *is* Adrian?' My mother turned to me then.

I said I had seen him at the bus-stop after church with his girlfriend and he had waved but I didn't know where he was going. He had had his guitar with him.

'Which girlfriend?' Mother asked.

'Anne-Marie.'

'She's an odd little creature, she is,' Mother said, but then she added, 'Bless her dear soul,' – and this was something she always said when she was about to criticize someone and then thought better of it; because in the Bible it says, 'Judge not, that thou be not judged'; and again in the Old Testament, 'the good man strikes not but heaps up coals of fire in Hell on the head of his enemy!'

While the older ones were taking forty winks, I went out to feed the rabbits. I picked dandelion-leaves and frosty spinach round the back where the curate's house was tagged on to the back of ours. We shared the same big garden. The rabbits were in two hutches by the steps that went up to the church vestry; a little suntrap it was, bright in the day's cold sunshine; and while I was stuffing in the food the curate came out from the vestry door and stood at the top of the steps in his long black cloak watching me.

'How are the little beggars getting on today then?' He laughed.

7

I said, okay.

He came down and took one in his arms, the white one called Peter that had turned out to be a female and given birth to eight more. I said the problem was I was really a bit too old to have rabbits now. I mean, I had got them when I was very young and everything and now they just kept living on and on and I had to keep feeding them, which was a pain because no one would ever want to buy a rabbit when it was already so old, and I had grown out of them.

He laughed still: he was very tall the Reverend Rolandson, blond-haired and blue-eyed with a straight nose and a great strong chin, and I remember when he first came to see my father for an interview my mother was very keen to have him because she said in the end it was nice to have a nice-looking fellow about the place and he would go down very well with the under-twenties, which was the future of the church when all was said and done. Perhaps at that time she was even thinking of pairing him off with Anna. Now though, in that long black cloak with the white rabbit held to his chest in the frosty sunshine, he looked very strange, Rolandson; he looked like a magician or a model, or someone in a film.

He said, 'I hope no one was offended by what I did this this morning. I've been praying about it ever since.'

I didn't know what to say.

'I really didn't have any choice though, to tell the truth. Quite suddenly the Lord just told me to do it.' He was looking at the rabbit which was twitching to be away now. The cages smelt a bit. 'The Lord's going to do great things for this church. Great things,' he said, and his voice was urgent and conspiratorial. He had great blond bushy eyebrows that lifted and fell as he spoke.

I took the rabbit from him and slipped it back in the cage

8

while he started brushing at all the white hairs that had stuck to his cloak.

'Bother!' he said, and then he said, 'Are you saved, Richard?' and I said yes, I was, and he said, 'But what about Adrian? He never comes to church, does he? Is he saved?' – and I said I didn't really know about Adrian, we never talked about it.

'The Lord is going to do something really marvellous here,' he told me. 'Marvellous. But the forces of Satan are legion.'

When I went back round the front of the house Ian was showing Anna his motorbike. He revved it up and took a turn round the front drive, and then Anna climbed on the pillion and he revved it up again and took another turn around the drive with her on the back and then my father came storming through the front door in a flaming temper and said if they wanted to make such an infernal racket why couldn't they go and do it elsewhere because he was trying to write his sermon and he needed a bit of peace and quiet. Under wiry black hair his cheeks and forehead would be boiling pink like salmon when he was angry and he would be holding an orange or an apple in his hand because he always ate fruit while he wrote his sermons. So Ian took Anna out on the street on the pillion which was what Mother had forbidden them to do and why they were stopping in the drive in the first place.

At tea, which was potato-cakes with butter, eaten on our laps, Father said he was sorry if he'd been a bit short previously, and Anna who always wanted to be in their good books finally brought the whole thing out then – wasn't it terrible what Roley had done this morning, she said, and wasn't he presumptive: he should join the Pentecostalists if he wanted to gabble rubbish like that. She sounded really outraged, more so even than my mother did when she talked about Rolandson. Ian said, with half a potato-cake still in his mouth, that there was a great deal of talk at the Missionary Training College about the charismatic movement but that the Principal thought it was all rubbish and codswallop.

My father though was very calm that evening. He took his glasses off and wiped them and put his fingers in his eyes. He had been praying about the problem for some long time he said, asking the Lord for guidance, and he said he thought when all was said and done we must keep our hearts and minds open to Christ's word of renewal, whatever source it came from, and must examine every new thing on its own merits and never never never be too proud to listen to anyone, however lowly. Everybody was subdued after that, and so I got up and took the dog out and I threw stones at the pigeons that settled on the lawn.

I told Mother I couldn't go to church in the evening because I had some homework I still hadn't done for tomorrow. She said I shouldn't leave my homework for the Lord's Day but she didn't really try to change my mind because they wanted me to do well at school. Everybody said I was a borderline case and I had to work very hard.

Adrian came in at nine with Anne-Marie before Father and Mother were back from the After Eight prayer meeting. They went straight upstairs to his room and then I tried to listen to them on the little intercom system I'd wired up between his room and mine by hanging wires out of the window and attaching them to a microphone behind his radiator: but I couldn't hear anything really, just the clicking of the radiator as the heat came on and went off and some very distant muffled voices and one loud thump. What did I expect to hear? I went to bed early and listened to Radio Moscow but then when I tried to go to sleep I couldn't for thinking what the Reverend Rolandson had done this morning, speaking in that gabbled voice and then talking to me about the forces of Satan being legion; but I wasn't exactly sure what 'legion' meant. I always felt a bit guilty, to tell the truth, at the end of Sundays, embarrassed and uneasy, so I took out my Bible and read a page at random and prayed. I wondered if perhaps I wasn't like one of those men of Gideon's who drank from their cupped hands and were always looking over their shoulders. Or if you didn't grow out of the church one day like you grew out of keeping rabbits.

★   ★   ★

In the week Adrian and Father had a terrible row and it only ended finally because Mother came in and wept so loud they couldn't go on. It actually started Tuesday night, I think, when Adrian came downstairs and found Anna and Ian whispering in the hall and he pretended not to know who Ian was because he had never actually been introduced before.

'Is there a telegram for me?' he asked, referring presumably to the motorbike. 'Dear Grandmother not dead at last, I don't suppose? We can't peal the jolly knell and revel in our inheritance?'

Anna got very upset by this kind of fun; so in a peeved voice she announced Ian's name and status. 'You're not the only one who has *friends*, you know,' she said, and Adrian said, 'Not a carnal relationship, I trust?' and he winked at Ian, who blushed through his freckles.

'Oh you!' Anna scowled. 'You think you're the bee's

knees, don't you!' and she stomped off into the lounge, leaving the red-faced Ian behind her. On the piano she banged out, 'Christian, can you see them, on your Holy Ground, / How the troops of Midian throng and throng around?' and Adrian left, shouting with laughter. Later, Anna said to Mother she thought it was demonic the way Adrian laughed sometimes, really fearful, as if he wasn't her brother at all but some other evil person.

Mother must have mentioned this to Father because the following evening when he and Adrian were playing chess together he brought it up, and he said Adrian shouldn't be too hard on Anna and me because we weren't that bright in the end, everybody knew that, but we were all still equal under God and we must learn how to treat each other with respect. Adrian and Father played chess together about once a week, whenever the one's being in coincided with the other's not having too much work to do. They were both very good at the game and a few years ago they had shared out the victories quite evenly, but now Adrian was getting better and winning almost very time. 'He has a mind like a scalpel,' Father used to say, 'really brilliant,' and he never complained when he lost but was rather proud of how clever his son was. So generally when they sat down together, bent over the board, Father with his big, bristling dark head almost touching Adrian's, which was smothered in very long, very blond hair, there was a general feeling of peace and reconciliation about the house and Mother said there was nothing she liked better than to see her husband and son playing together and having fun. It did her heart good, she said: she used to peep in at them through the lounge door a moment and then hurry off, as if her prolonged presence might somehow jeopardize this blessed peace.

Adrian chewed at the space between his thumb and first

finger and when Father moved he moved immediately afterwards, and rapidly, and Father said, 'Hah! Yes, of course! Hah, clever devil you!' and he tugged at his earlobes which were red and hairy. 'You clever clever devil!' Then between games he brought up this business about Anna, and Adrian said, yes, he was the first person to agree that everybody had equal rights, whether you believed in God or not, and that was why he could never understand why they wouldn't let him give up maths and physics and study music instead like he wanted to. This was an old argument that always made Father furious and he said there could be absolutely no connection between the one issue and the other, and it was folly, but pure, absolute, complete folly, for Adrian to go and throw away all the intelligence he had to do something un-academic and unrewarding like music, especially modern music; and in his anger he began to bang the wooden pieces back into their places for the next game. It was downright ridiculous, he said, 'Stupefying!'

Adrian smiled and he said, 'Temper, temper.'

Father was livid then and shouted that he, Adrian, should think twice before being cheeky to his father and he should realize that according to the law he was still a minor and the responsibility of his elders and betters, and just because he could beat his father at chess didn't mean he knew what was best for him in this world, because experience was a different thing from intelligence. They both shouted at each other now and Adrian said, in the end, for all their talk about Christianity and spirituality, he and my mother were just as materialist as anybody else and entirely conditioned by the shallow society they'd grown up in; they wanted him to do engineering or something just to make a lot of money. Father was furious and in his frustration he slapped Adrian hard around the head, sweeping all the pieces off the chess-board at the same time; but Adrian remained perfectly still and smiled the little cynical smile he always seemed to have ready these days, the lips curling up around clenched teeth, the jaw thrust right out – so confident Adrian was – and then Mother came in and wept and she said they would bring her down with grey hairs to the grave with all their arguing, and through her tears she told Adrian he didn't know how lucky he was having parents like he did; he should find out what some of the parents of his friends were like; and she clung to Father, weeping. Adrian banged out of the room and Anna watched him up the stairs, gloating from the dining-room door. Because Anna was jealous of the relationship Adrian had with Father when they bent their heads together over the chess-board and nobody was supposed to disturb them for hours and hours.

In my room Adrian said, 'So what do you think, Ricky boy?' He was matey.

I didn't say anything. I used to sit by my window with my feet on the radiator watching the main road beyond our gravel drive, and I had a pair of old binoculars for trying to see the people in the block of flats beyond, but I never saw anything.

'They're really loopy – they're living in another century, you know. They haven't got the first idea what the world's like today.'

'No,' I said.

'And then they go and talk about experience! That Anna's a pig too, watching television and eating biscuits all evening, a face-ache is what she is. And this boyfriend, Christ, what a jerk, what a dud! Singing those stupid choruses together.' He kicked the wall by my bed. 'Jesus!'

'They'll be sending up burnt offerings next!' he said.

'They're welcome to my rabbits any time,' I said.

He laughed. 'Want to come and have a game of Risk or something?' he asked, so we went and played Risk and his room was full of guitars and bits of guitars and little sculptures that he'd glued together from cigarette packets; he smoked, which he never dared to do downstairs, and put some progressive music on very loud so that after a while my mother came upstairs and banged hard on the door and then went away without opening it. She didn't open it of course because she didn't want to have an argument with Adrian about his smoking.

★   ★   ★

Three weeks later my father announced to my mother in bed that he had been Baptized in the Spirit and spoken in tongues and felt the Lord move within him; and this was the same week Anna said she was going to marry Ian and go to China, and that Adrian was expelled from his school.

Father told Mother the point was he'd finally understood 1 Corinthians 12 to 14, and he told the congregation the same thing on Sunday morning. His voice was strangely thick with a sort of love and excitement and he smiled constantly, which was unusual for him. His cheeks and forehead shone with the heat of it and his dark hair bristled up, because whenever he was excited he would push his hand through it and grip it there in a bunch. He told them there really were Gifts of the Spirit, supernatural gifts, to give the church an edge and to overcome the frustration he had suffered from his entire life, the frustration of one's powerlessness in the face of Satan. He said there was a literal real tongue of flame sent by God to kindle all our hearts and gird up our loins to greater things: 'Yea, even unto miracles,' he said, 'even unto

15

miracles and martyrdom.' The Reverend Rolandson said ay-men quite incessantly and when we sang the final hymn, which was 'Breathe on me, Breath of God', he lifted his arms again, both together, as he had done that other Sunday, and turned toward the stained-glass window – only this week there was no sunshine.

Then after the blessing Father said those who had to go or wanted to, should go now, but he was going to hold a meeting immediately for all those who wanted to hear more about the Gifts of the Spirit and the Baptism of Fire in the power of Our Lord and Master. An uneasy shuffling filled the church then and about half the people scrambled to their feet but about half of them stayed put, because it was an active kind of church with lots of under-twenties and my father was very popular and considered quite modern because he had introduced singing with the guitar on the chancel steps and he always went over for a game of ping-pong when the Youth Fellowship met on Saturday nights. Naturally, from the back my mother could see who went and who stayed and she sat there still and slightly confused-looking, blinking her big eyelashes in the kind pale face she had. She was quite a beautiful woman, my mother, with glinting honey hair just threaded here and there with silver and wide generous lips. Then she leaned to me and sighed and said, 'You'd better pop back home and switch off the oven and take Susie out before she gets desperate.' Susie was the dog. So I dashed out while she went on to her knees.

That meeting must have lasted a good three hours in the cold, windy church and there must have been many a roast ruined I suppose for the sake of hearing precisely what my father and the Reverend Rolandson meant by the Gifts of the Spirit and the Baptism of Fire. Adrian came down in his bell-bottoms and the Indian smock he had bought at Camden

Lock and he was annoyed that lunch was late because he had to go out this afternoon. 'They're all loopy,' he said, 'nuts,' and then when Ian arrived he snorted and went back upstairs and played his electric guitar very loud.

Ian said he didn't know what to think. He stood beside the radiator and scratched his freckled ears. To tell the truth he didn't like it, he said, this charismatic stuff. Although he respected my father very much. But if you started talking about miracles and gabbling in tongues it just made it harder for the unbeliever to believe, and especially the Chinese, he said, who had been brought up with communism. We weren't Buddhists after all or anything like that, were we, going into trances and so on. He zipped and unzipped his black motorbike jacket, standing with his back to the radiator. I said I didn't know; I hadn't gone to the meeting because of the dog and the roast and I didn't really know what any of it meant.

'We were going to tell your dad we were getting engaged today. Do you think he'll mind?'

For some reason, I remember, I wasn't at all surprised. I don't know why. I said I thought not and I opened my manual on audio-electronics and made a big show of reading it.

'About our wanting to go to China, I mean. We want to go together.'

'Not as long as you don't go on your motorbike, I suppose.'

'No – the roads are too bad after India,' he said. 'I've given up the idea of going overland.'

Anna, Mother and Father came back together and they were very dignified and quiet, only I could see my mother had been crying because of the stains there still were on her cheeks, and her red eyes. Adrian came down and we ate quite calmly then with even one or two jokes and the only unusual thing was, at the end, before we got down, Father said could we bow our heads in prayer together.

'Almighty God, Our Father,' he began. Instead of bowing his head, Adrian propped his chin on his fists and kept his eyes open and stared hard at me across the table. I felt it and glanced up at him and then down again and he was grinning a great big broad grin and chewing at a strand of his hair. My sister's face instead was waxy smooth and concentrated and devout.

'Almighty Father, we petition Thee today to breathe on us all here Thy ever new and Holy Spirit which Thou hast sent abroad in this land. And may it not bring divisions between us Dear Lord, but oh, let Satan be kept far hence from our midst.' He paused. 'Ay-men,' Anna whispered just a little uncertainly, and Mother said, 'Ah-men.' Adrian drummed lightly with his long white fingers on the table.

'And we would petition Thee now also, for Your children, our loved ones, Anna and Ian, as they prepare to pledge themselves each to the other and both to You, that You would make them strong together and and show them where their duty lies, whether it be here in the humdrum of our modern life, or far far away in other lands claiming new souls for Thy name.'

I was surprised how generous Father was to Ian, because I was sure, deep down he didn't think much of him at all. I glanced up quickly and there was Adrian opposite, still staring at me, those eyes like coals, and he bared his teeth in a little grin of mockery, the little cynical grin he had.

'Mind if I push off?' he said as soon as Father had finished. 'Got to be abroad in the world myself, and I'm already late.'

My father was perfectly calm. 'Not at all,' he said. 'It's a free country. You are perfectly at liberty to come and go as you please, laddie.'

'Thank you, sir,' Adrian said, and he stomped out of the room. He has a club foot, Adrian, twisted and shrunken, so he limps and walks with a roll, and when he is angry or sarcastic he accentuates this limp by stomping – I don't know why – but somehow it seems to work; it seems full of malignance somehow. He stomped; my mother drew in and held a long deep breath and as soon as he'd gone Anna said, 'Sometimes! That brother of mine! I could wring his neck!'

Then that next Thursday he was expelled from school. He was caught smoking cannabis with two friends in the cricket nets so they scarcely had any choice really, and it was very embarrassing for Father because this was a church school and he was the chaplain. They had a furious row about it in the study and Adrian said he was quite happy to be expelled because now he could apply to a sixth-form college to do his A-levels in music and art. Father said no he damn-well couldn't, he could do no such thing, and for my father to use even a word as strong as 'damn', it was something you only heard once a year in our house. Mother sat in the dining-room knitting grimly with the dog at her feet and a Bible on her lap, whispering to herself. Anna was out at an Under-Twenties prayer meeting with Ian, even though she was twenty-one.

I said to my mother, 'What exactly is cannabis?'

'A drug,' she said.

'I know, but I mean, what does it do?'

She said, 'Why do you want to know?'

'Just curious. Everybody's talking about it so much.'

She was silent a moment, counting stitches, and then we both could hear Father's voice raised in the other room

19

saying he was fed up to the very back teeth of being answered back at: he was head of the family and he was going to assert his authority! The dog whined and pawed at Mother's leg.

'The point is, it's evil,' she said, and then she started to say the same things she used to say about strikes and communism; that there were a lot of people about who were determined to disrupt our way of life as it was at the moment and these were the kind of people who spread unrest and communism and sold drugs; and it was just a terrible shame, she said, with tears coming into her eyes, a terrible terrible shame, that Adrian was foolish enough to mix with these kind of people; and a lot of the problem was that fearful, horrible music he listened to which was entirely controlled by the same disruptive group.

At which moment a door slammed and Adrian stomped out of the study: he put on his long Afghan coat and the woolly cap with the scarf attached and he slammed the front door as well, as hard as he could.

'Stupefying!' my father muttered going past the dining-room to the lavatory.

I stayed up late that night doing my homework and when I went to bed and passed my parents' door, I stopped and listened. There was a low murmuring, a hissing sound coming from the room, and when I listened very carefully with my ear nearly against the door I could distinguish that same babble of sounds without words that had issued from Rolandson's mouth in the chancel a month ago. And then I knew that they were using the Sword of the Spirit to pray for Adrian, my mother and my father both, because Mother had come round – and for some reason I felt woefully, impossibly guilty, and afraid.

★ ★ ★

Donald Rolandson had been Baptized in the spirit at a 'Renewal Meeting', held by a certain Joy Kandinsky, an American woman from Arkansas: she had layed her hands on his head and he had spoken in tongues and felt the power of the Lord move within him and the Holy Spirit burn in his heart. He was quite frank and open about it and said it had been the most incredible experience of his life: hence he had persuaded Father to go and see her and this was where he first spoke in tongues too and where he learnt to say ay-men as well, like Rolandson did. So began the heady period of 'Renewal', and before very long there were trips arranged by the church to take coachloads to listen to Joy Kandinsky where she preached in a large marquee near Bournemouth on the property of an aristocrat who was one of her converts. She layed hands on people and everybody layed hands on each other and everybody spoke in tongues, which was that strange babble of words without words, and they raised their arms during hymns – and then to some also, according to the Holy Scriptures, were given the gifts of Prophecy and of Words of Wisdom, and to others the gifts of Healing and of Interpretation, and the gift also of the Casting out of Demons.

So the whole church changed – and Mother and Father changed likewise, and Anna changed with them as she always would. Previously the situation had seemed so stable and sound: Matins and Evensong; Christmas, Epiphany and Easter and all the long Sundays after Trinity, year in year out; Father preached the Gospel and got a new curate every three years and there was snooker and table-tennis at the youth-club and the routine quite endless, endless women's meetings my mother took; Monday Night at Eight, the Mothers' Union, the Thursday Coffee Group, Young Wives and so on – and finally, every spring, there was the Annual General Meeting of the PCC where Father used to row with everybody about their commitment to evangelism and try to have more money allotted to Oxfam and less to the restoration of the fabric, because the fabric always seemed in a state of constant and galloping disrepair however much you spent on it, he said; and there would be bad feeling for two or three weeks between him and the people who wanted to mend the roof.

But now all this changed and every moment became alive with change; because now in any meeting, formal or informal, administrative, social or religious, somebody might break out in tongues, kneel suddenly, with a torrent of words that weren't words, hands uplifted and trembling; or there might be a Prophecy, or a Word of Wisdom, or somebody would claim to have a deep spiritual sickness and call for the laying-on-of-hands, and my father or Donald Rolandson would hold their arms outstretched with the palms of their hands just over the person's head, and everybody would pray together in low, muttering tones: 'Oh Lord, be Thou with this poor soul now, even in his darkest hour, and invest him with Thy power, fill him with Thy Spirit.' This 'everybody', strangely enough, was still almost exactly the same congregation as always, bar a few who hadn't been able to stomach it; still the same doctors and businessmen, the same civil servants and respectable middle-class women, praising the Lord and speaking in tongues and raising their arms in the air whenever they sang a hymn; because this was a well-to-do suburb where the Sword of the Spirit and the Holy Dove had come home to roost.

On Sunday morning, Anna substituted the choruses of Joy Kandinsky for those of Billy Graham and so now she sang 'Raised on a Dove's Wings', and 'Thou Art Worthy', and seventy or eighty per cent of the congregation raised their arms as they joined in and closed their eyes in beatific smiles and swayed from side to side in ecstasy. Then Father continued with the 1666 prayer-book as usual and a service as formal as you might find in any ecclesiastical church – because he was determined, he said, that this was a 'Renewal' of the old, and not a replacement. 'Renewal' was an important word, he said, subtly different from 'Revival': because 'Revival' implied they had been dead beforehand, which they most certainly hadn't been; whereas 'Renewal' implied a new gift from God – and after church now he would continue this kind of debate at lunch-time, speaking about Satan and the Lord over the roast in the same familiar tones he used to use before for talking about Harold Wilson and Sir Alec Douglas-Home.

But everybody was talking about Satan. Rolandson was talking about him almost non-stop, and I remember he said at the Youth Fellowship on Saturday how Satan was present in the words and music of certain progressive pop groups, called Black Widow and Black Sabbath, who sang about witches and black masses: so all the members of the Youth Fellowship who had bought records by these groups had to bring them into the meetings over the next weeks and have them smashed to smithereens in front of everybody, and the debris was put in the incinerator behind the vestries while we all sang 'Raised on a Dove's Wing' together, standing on the patch of gravel there in the howling wind.

The church started going out more into the community too, buttonholing people on the High Road on Saturday morning, taking their own tent in the Spring Carnival with three or four services each evening, and sending out nightly parties to knock at every front door in the neighbourhood and invite people to our church. 'The Lord is doing great works in our midst,' Donald Rolandson said, and when he said it he used to rub his hands together and grin out of all his big handsome face, like a young American who has just made his first million dollars. But this was what Joy Kandinsky did too. 'The Lord is doing great works in our midst,' he said. 'The Latter Days are upon us.'

The groups that went out knocking on people's doors were called 'Soul-Searching Parties', because they were supposed to be searching out souls for God. I went with them sometimes, but when I did I was always afraid we would run into Adrian on the street, with his Afghan coat and club foot and the cynical small grin. Every new street we turned into I used to look up and down, everywhere, for his blond hair and headband, because there was nothing I feared more than to run into Adrian while I was on a Soul-Searching Party, nothing, I don't think, not even Hell itself. So I went out on the streets with a small group of others, talking about Christ and watching all the time for Adrian; but at the school I went to in town I never said a word about Christianity, never mind the Holy Spirit, and I laughed at the same jokes all the others did and at the back of the class with some friends we started a collection of all the girls who appeared everyday on page three of the *Sun*, and we pasted them in a scrapbook.

★   ★   ★

My mother had always joined in with my father in his work and one of the special aspects of her 'ministry' was that she counselled young women who found themselves in trouble of some kind or other; so sometimes when I got home from school in the afternoon she was shut in the lounge with someone and there would be sounds of low voices or tears and dinner would be late. She was particularly well-adapted to this work, I suppose, because she was very sympathetic and had an extraordinary patience when it came to listening to other people's stories, something my father didn't have. She would sit forward with her small pale hands pressed together over her lips and her attention seemed to be absolute and every minute or so she would say 'yes, yes', in a quiet generous way to keep the other person talking. In fact I have heard her speak on the phone in this way and say nothing more than 'yes, yes', at perfectly regular intervals for upwards of half an hour; and with her body in the same attitude too, leant forward, the hand not holding the phone pressed to the side of her mouth and her brown wide eyes staring with attention as if directly into the eyes of another. Then, if Adrian was in the room, he would begin to say 'no, no', every time my mother said 'yes, yes' – 'yes, yes', 'no, no', 'yes, yes', 'no, no' – and instead of getting angry she smiled, and when finally she put the phone down she burst out laughing and said, 'What a silly girl, I ask you. Dearie me!' But she was always very kind to 'her girls', as she called them, and very confidential, and she never told any of us about the mess that any of them were in. 'Marilyn's in a terrible mess, bless her dear heart,' she used to say, or Susan or Mary, but she never told us what the mess was. She never even told Father, I don't think.

Now that the Holy Spirit had arrived though, there seemed to be more and more of these girls, and more and more often dinner would be late. Father said it was because Mother had been given the gift of Wisdom and Perception to see into the souls of others and the Lord was sending her people on purpose to solve their problems and to bring them into His fold. And her methods changed too. She didn't talk any more about advice or counselling, but about freeing their spirits and healing them and even, later, about casting demons out of them. So now when I came back from school, sweaty in my Terylene trousers and with my plastic brief-case, it wasn't just low voices or tears I heard, but howls sometimes and screams, throbbing from behind the pepper-mint door of our lounge, real screams. Then when this happened Anna used to play 'Raised on a Dove's Wings' on the piano in the hall, with little trills on the treble part of the keyboard, and she prayed out loud, and if my father was about he would phone up Rolandson next door and tell him to pray too, because my mother was striving with Satan and Satan was howling.

'Go upstairs and pray,' he said to me, 'that the Lord may do great things.' He seemed distracted and nervous as if not quite sure of himself, and I kicked off my shoes on the parquet flooring and shot up the stairs three at a time in my sweaty socks. But I didn't pray. I clamped my headphones on my ears and tried to find Radio Moscow on my home-made short-wave radio, because I couldn't bear to listen to the howls and cries coming from beneath or to the rise and fall of Mother's voice babbling in that language that was not a language and my sister trilling on the piano and reciting 1 Corinthians 12 out loud. Then Radio Moscow said the Americans had committed appalling atrocities in Vietnam and the whole Western World was in the throes of deca-dence and facing a complete collapse of moral standards; and while I listened I watched out of the window with my old binoculars, but the people in the flats opposite all had thick curtains hung across their windows and never a crack.

One of Mother's 'girls' came to live with us. Maggie. She was a jolly-looking young cockney woman, broad-shouldered with fiercely hennaed hair which she wore in a tired perm and she was a sergeant, apparently, in the Metropolitan Police Training Department. Mother didn't tell us what her problem was, except that it was a big one, bless her dear heart, a very big one. Still, Maggie seemed cheerful enough. She set out very jauntily every morning in her crisp blue uniform, always ready with a bright hello or a jokey remark and she slept in the guest room next to Adrian's. After a month or so, rather surprisingly, she and Adrian became the best of friends.

'Maggie has made friends with Adrian,' Anna told my mother while they baked together. On Friday evening they used to bake all the cakes for the rest of the week. 'I saw them going out together yesterday – with Anne-Marie too.'

'That's nice,' Mother said.

'To the pub, I shouldn't be surprised, knowing Adrian.' Anna had a constant frown on her face while she worked and used to bite her bottom lip. She was especially good at making chocolate éclairs.

'That's not the end of the world,' Mother said with perfect equanimity; so I thought it couldn't be alcoholism that was Maggie's problem, like it was with some of the other girls.

'I think Adrian's laugh is positively demonic sometimes, the way he does it,' Anna said, and she said, 'Sometimes it hardly seems like he's my brother at all but somebody else.'

'No, he doesn't have a very nice laugh, does he,' Mother said.

I scraped the empty basin of cake mix and ate it off the edge of a plastic spatula.

'But what I can't see is, if she's been saved and Baptized in the Spirit and so on, how on earth can she put up with Adrian and his friends and the kind of horrible things they say?'

'Perhaps she likes him,' Mother said. 'Worse things have befallen us, Anna love.'

So then I thought, Maggie couldn't be a nymphomaniac either, or Mother would be worried about Adrian having sex with her; because one of the things that worried Mother most, I think, was that Adrian might be having sex with one of the many girls he went round with, and that was why she never, never went into his room when he had a girl there – never. She never even stopped to listen by his door but walked quickly right by.

Then Mother said to me, 'Where is Adrian this evening, by the way, Richard?'

'Out with Anne-Marie,' I said, and Anna snorted.

'And do you actually know anything about Anne-Marie, who she is, what she does and so on?'

So I told them Anne-Marie was from Hampstead and her father was a lawyer and she went to the same sixth-form college as Adrian and studied music too, only her instrument was the flute. My mother said that was nice. Also she spoke French, I said, because her mother was French; but I didn't tell them the other thing Adrian had told me about her, that she had the best small pointed tits in the world and she didn't wear a bra – ever.

Anna said, 'She buys her clothes from Oxfam shops.'

Mother laughed: there were these evenings when Mother was determined to be light-hearted and others when she worried and fretted over everything. 'At least it all goes to a good cause,' she said, 'bless her dear heart.' And she asked Anna about Ian.

'Ian's okay,' Anna said, not looking up from where she was rolling out puff-pastry, and my mother turned her head and winked at me.

If Maggie wasn't an alcoholic or a nymphomaniac then I wasn't quite sure what her problem might be, and I spent a long time thinking about it and I even thought I might put a microphone round the windows and behind her radiator, only it was too far from my room to hers and I was a bit scared of being caught. She was always very pleasant to me, Maggie, and she was always telling me with her heavy cockney accent how my parents were wonderful and how the Lord had been, 'really smashin' ' to her. But Maggie was pleasant to everybody, always, and on the evenings she didn't go out with Adrian and Anne-Marie she used to stand by the piano where my sister played, one hand resting lightly on her shoulder and singing along with her 'Raised on a Dove's Wings', and 'Thou Art Worthy', and another hymn that was popular now called 'And Should It Be'. She had a biggish body with heavy breasts that sagged in the thick sweaters she wore and she always had tight jeans on, so that the lines of her knickers showed because her bottom was a bit fat. But her face was nice and round and cheerful and she was always laughing from it or grinning with a mischievous grin. I remember one night when I stayed up late trying to increase the amplification on my radio, I heard laughter, her laughter, coming from outside, and peeping through a crack in the curtains I saw a little group coming in through the main gate: three of them, Maggie, Adrian and Anne-Marie, their faces all yellow in the cellophane-yellow light of the streetlamp just beyond our drive. And the odd thing was, Maggie and Anne-Marie had both picked up Adrian, making a kind of chair with their crossed hands and they were both kissing him at the same time, each side of his yellow face, giggling together in that strange city light with him grinning his small cynical grin. And from where I watched too, it seemed as though, with his arms round their two necks, his hands were covering one each of their breasts; and they giggled very loud, and stumbled and swayed wildly from side to side, him grabbing and flailing, until finally they dropped him.

I went to bed and read my Bible for more than an hour, chapter after chapter, and I read that verse that says, 'If thou art hot with love for me I will bless thee and cherish thee, and if thou art cold I will seek thee out and save thee; but if thou art luke-warm for me, behold, I will spit thee from my mouth and hide my face from thee and there will be weeping and gnashing of teeth.' So then I thought, surely I was worse than Anna, because I wasn't hot, and in a way worse even than Adrian, because I wasn't cold; so I prayed and prayed and I made a huge effort to speak in tongues, but nothing would come out of my mouth: I felt nothing inside myself. It made me desperate, this feeling nothing inside myself, and I wondered if perhaps I should get up and go and ask my father to lay hands on me that minute, which was what they all wanted me to do of course, but I didn't do it. I don't know why, but I couldn't. I didn't want to. I couldn't bear the thought of them all jabbering away around me with those words that weren't words and my mother ecstatic and happy and my father generous and happy. So I went to sleep wallowing in guilt and thinking of Adrian's hands clawing at those two women's breasts, the one of them small and pointed and the other full and heavy and hanging, and I dreamt of the Devil and all kinds of lewd things.

★   ★   ★

Although he could be very sentimental and passionate, and then dictatorial in the church or hot-tempered at home, my father's spirit was basically a quiet, and above all a theoretical one; and so now the Holy Ghost had arrived in our midst he had begun to spend a lot of his spare time theorizing about just what this might mean and making files full of notes, because he wanted to write a book about it called, *The Sword We Must Hold High*.

'The point is,' he said at dinner when he aired his views – he was silent at breakfast and lunch but at dinner-time generally he aired his views – 'the point is that the Devil is making a great push these days and the Lord has sent His Spirit so that we will be able to combat this evil with the proper weapons – a kind of escalation of spiritual warfare, if you like,' he said, and he used the words the television used everyday about Vietnam. My father liked to talk in this way, as if he was some kind of professional general, and on the wall above the cooker he hung a Scripture Union text on a red scroll which said 'AS THY DAYS, SO SHALL THY STRENGTH BE.' Mother explained to me that this meant, depending on the era you lived in, that is, whether Satan was strong or weak, so the Lord would send you the strength you required to combat him – which was Father's explanation of why the Sword of the Spirit hadn't been put into our hands until 1968. But I couldn't help thinking this text simply meant that when you got old you'd probably be fairly weak, and I remember I had to make a very big mental effort to understand it the way Father saw it; like the effort you have to make when you've drawn a cube on a piece of paper and you want to make one corner come to the front rather than another. But anyway, because Father had glued it above the cooker, the scroll kept falling off because of the steam there, so he glued it on the opposite wall but it fell off there too because that wall had damp in it and the PCC always said they hadn't enough money to have it repaired because of the amount Father had allotted to missions and charities overseas; and so in the end, I suppose, he got fed up with fishing it up off the floor and simply tore it up and threw it away, because after a certain point I never saw it again.

The increasing strength of Satan in our present time, Father went on at dinner, was manifested in particular in the following people, nations and things: Chairman Mao, the Russians, the Vietnamese, the left-wing of the Labour Party, the unions, drugs, pornography, sex outside marriage, and certain types of modern music. There were also a number of other things which, though not definitely in this camp, were to be considered equivocal and suspect. These were, very long hair (in men), the word, 'psychedelic', abstract paintings, and students' unions.

So then after Father had aired his views, he and Adrian would start arguing about them because of course Adrian supported the Vietnamese and the Labour Party and the unions whenever there was a strike and all kinds of modern music. 'Communism is inspired by Satan – Mao is an Antichrist,' my father said, and Adrian used to say things like, 'Oh, what's the date, by the way? 30th March 1868, isn't it? No, heavens! Of course, it's *1968*! I *am* sorry, I almost had the wrong century there! Could happen to anybody though.' And my father used to say. 'You can make fun of me all you like, laddie, but you'll never turn black into white, oh no!' Then my mother would say things like, 'Oh dear, have we run out of salt, Anna? I do hope we haven't' – because all she wanted to do was change the subject.

'Their so-called "abstraction" is the deliberate irrationalism of Lucifer,' Father said, referring to some painters Adrian had probably been praising.

'Well, I suppose that must make me pretty well entirely demonic then,' Adrian said with great resignation, flashing that cynical smile around clenched teeth, and my sister said, 'You've said it, mate.'

'Because I really don't want to have to traipse up to Sainsbury's and do a great shop tomorrow,' Mother said. 'Let me see now, perhaps there's some still left in the posh cruet in the lounge.'

Then if they'd managed to avoid an almighty row, Father and Adrian would go off into the lounge to play chess, leaving Anna and I to wash up while Mother made the coffee. And Anna was more jealous than ever that Father spent so much time playing chess with Adrian and that he said more and more often that Adrian's mind was like a scalpel.

She said, 'Sometimes, I don't know how he can go and sit with that brother of mine after he's been so downright cheeky.'

And she said, 'I don't know how he can stomach him, because I'm sure I can't.'

'He should get that stupid hair cut,' she said. 'It's filthy the way he chews it all the time.'

'They just like a good argument sometimes,' Mother said mildly, and she was happy because Adrian and Father were playing quietly together again and had stopped talking about the Antichrist and Joe Gormley and the Vietnamese.

'He never does anything about the house. He thinks he's the bee's knees with those stupid Oxfam clothes.'

'He's just growing up,' Mother said, pouring the coffee. But Anna was trembling.

'And the way he laughs at me sometimes, it's positively demonic. You wouldn't think he was my brother at all.'

Then as soon as Mother had gone to take the coffee to the others, Anna wailed and burst into tears over the sink and then she lifted her hands out all wet from the dishes and threw them round me and hugged me.

'It's off with Ian!' she sobbed. 'All off!'

I tried to mutter I was sorry.

'I'm not going to get married now, never, ever ever!' – and she buried her long dark hair in my shoulders, snivelling. But I couldn't think what to say.

After a little she recovered and lifted her face. She has a thin face like mine, Anna, only now her cheeks were red and puffy with tears and the patches of acne she had, and her grey eyes were rimmed with hard red.

'Anyway, he wasn't that clever. And he was never baptized in the Spirit. He said it was stupid. He said we were all stupid for praying in tongues and it was just stupid gibberish.' She sighed, then said, 'And Father never liked him really. He never liked any of my boyfriends because he thinks they're all thick and he thinks Adrian's so clever-clever who's such a pig!'

She burst into tears again on my shoulder with her damp hands round my back, really weeping and weeping, and she said, 'You don't despise me, do you, Ricky? Please say you don't, say you don't, oh please! Because all the others despise me, I know. They think I've got spots and I'm thick and useless. Please say you don't depise me!'

But I didn't say anything. I was always struck completely dumb by other people's emotions and I couldn't say anything at all.

At night, towards eleven, my parents always had cocoa and Ritz biscuits together on the kitchen table and this was one of their quiet meals, almost as quiet as breakfast. There would be great long silences of five or even ten minutes with the only sound being the slow long sucking sound Mother and Father made when they drank their cocoa, because they were two people who could never drink hot drinks silently. When we were a bit younger and Adrian used to come to these

suppers he used to start making the same slurping, sucking
sound they did and putting on the same utterly blank face
they both would have at the end of the day, wide eyes and
slack lips – but they didn't notice. And the louder he sucked
and slurped and the longer they didn't notice, the more
hilarious it became, and sometimes all we three children
would be positively heaving and splitting our sides with
laughter, until finally one of us couldn't hold it in anymore
and would burst out laughing, spluttering cocoa all across the
table and over the plate of Ritz crackers and the dry Edam
cheese my mother always bought because it was the
cheapest.

'It's high time you young scallywags went to bed,' Father
said then, never understanding the joke. 'You're overtired,
the pack of you'; and he would make us bow our heads while
he said that blessing, his favourite, 'And now unto Him who
is able to keep you without stumbling and without stain . . .'
and then we were herded off to bed so that they could
continue, sipping and sucking their cocoa in peace.

But tonight Father said, 'Where's Anna, by the way?'
because Anna normally came to these suppers and sometimes they went into the lounge afterwards and sang a
doxology together, with Anna playing the piano and doing
her little trills on the treble part while Father stood behind
her with his hands on her shoulders: in fact those were the
times Father was most emotional and talked almost in tears
about his love for his family and God and sometimes one of
them spoke in tongues while Mother was in the kitchen
boiling the water for our hot-water bottles.

'I don't know, love,' Mother said. She turned to me,
'Where is Anna?'

'Over at Rolandson's prayer meeting,' I said.

It was a bit late for her still to be over there, Father said.

'She's broken off with Ian,' I said. 'She seemed a bit depressed.'

'I was wondering when that would happen,' Mother said. She barely even interrupted the rhythm of her supping.

His mouth full of crackers, Father only grunted.

'And was she very upset?'

I said she had gone upstairs and sat with Maggie in her room for a bit and then they had both gone to Roley's prayer meeting which he was holding every night this week to pray for the Church behind the Iron Curtain.

'With Maggie?' Mother asked, and then suddenly her face changed. She went quite white.

'Yes,' I said.

'But the meeting should have finished ages ago!' She shot a glance at my father, and already she was thrusting back her chair quite violently. She tore off her apron and was out of the kitchen and scrambling down the few steps to the front door in an instant. Father wiped his mouth and hurried after.

Then a few minutes later they came back with Anna and Maggie together. Anna was still snivelling into Father's arms. Maggie was saying, 'There in't nothin' to worry about, Mrs Bowen, nothin' at all. We were just 'avin' a little natter out there in the garden, what with her breaking up with her fiancé an' all and bein' so upset.' But my mother was tight-lipped.

And I couldn't fathom it at all.

*   *   *

I finally got my microphone to work, the one that went behind the radiator in Adrian's room. I stepped up the power of the amplifier and reduced the distortion by using more

36

transistors – I read how to do it in a book – and so it was I heard everything they did one evening when everybody else was out at church and the radiators weren't on because it was so mild. I heard everything they did.

Then I was so guilty and confused after hearing this, so utterly confused and lost and stained, frantic almost, because I loved Adrian and in some ways I wanted to be like him, that the following evening I cut the wires between the two windows and I went into Adrian's room to take the microphone away from behind his radiator. But it had got lodged quite firmly back there, jammed between the wall and a pipe and I couldn't prise the thing out. I forced my arm right down between the wall and the radiator, squeezing and hurting my elbow, and still I could only touch it with the tips of two fingers. It wouldn't come. And so while I was still struggling to get at the thing, Adrian came in and discovered it all.

He hit me really hard with his open hand about my head and I stumbled and fell back against the wall. His eyes were hard grey-blue and his jaw pushed out.

'You creepy little bastard!' he hissed. 'You snot-rag!' But when he hit me he wasn't in a temper and frustrated like Father would be. He was just cold and angry.

'You little pervert,' he said. 'You're worse than them. At least they're honest.'

I was trembling. It was only an experiment, I said, only an experiment; I promised, I swore it, an audio-experiment; and I was only just setting it up, honestly honestly; I hadn't heard anything, nothing at all. My head really hurt because Adrian wore big rings on his hands and one of them had caught me round the ear. The blood seemed pricking from the pores of my skin there and I felt sick.

'What did you expect to hear?' he shouted. 'A black bloody

mass or something? You think I'm a demon like the rest of them?'

Adrian usually has a pale, nearly white face. But now his cheeks were livid. He was so angry. He hissed in mockery and made a sort of magical evil gesture with his arms outstretched and fingers quivering like somebody casting a spell. Then he burst out laughing.

'Oh just get the fuck out of here,' he said, and I scrambled to my feet and away. I could have hit him back of course, because with his club foot he was quite easy to unbalance, but I didn't. The way he laughed scared me.

And now in the corridor I ran into my mother with a duster and she could see at once I'd been crying and I was covering my ear with my hand.

'What did he do to you?' she demanded.

'Why are you crying, what did he do? I want you to tell me this minute.'

'Nothing,' I said. I felt so sick.

'He must have done something, laddie,' she said, borrowing Father's voice. 'I don't imagine you're crying for absolutely nothing. So what was it?'

I said I'd slipped and banged my head on the radiator.

'A likely story,' she said. She looked at me, angry but hesitant. 'I heard voices raised,' – and then she walked very briskly and purposefully toward Adrian's room, but at the closed door she stopped. She stood there rigid a moment and then turned to the airing cupboard which was behind and pulled out a heap of towels. 'I'll get your father to deal with this,' she said. 'He'll soon sort out what's what.'

But she never did. She never spoke to Father about it at all. Because she never spoke to Father about anything like this in the end, for the trouble it would cause.

*　　*　　*

38

So for the next few weeks I felt terribly guilty and in my mind I heard over and again those sounds I'd heard in Adrian's room – I couldn't get them out of my mind – and I started going to every church service and to all Rolandson's prayer meetings, and I even started going on the Soul-Searching Parties again, but I didn't feel any better: I just couldn't get it out of my mind, the exciting thing I'd heard in that room. I tried to speak in tongues on my own at night because it seemed now, according to what was said in church, that if you didn't speak in tongues you weren't really a proper Christian and God hadn't blessed you. I read 1 Corinthians 12 to 14 and a little book Father was always recommending called *Baptized in the Spirit – A Handbook*, but all I managed to come out with was two guttural words, sibilant and fake and chopped-sounding, and always the same, 'Ravishnah, homorrah homorrah. Ravishnah, homorrah homorrah.' Then I was so shocked at the sound and feel of these ugly words in my mouth – 'Ravishnah, homorrah homorrah' – so horrified in fact, that I stayed up all night reading instead of going to sleep; only now I had said them I couldn't get rid of them, I couldn't get those words out of my mind. While I read they came back and back to my mouth, garbled and full of breath and effort – 'Ravishnah, homorrah homorrah!' – and while I drowsed a little as I read they got mixed up somehow with those fierce sounds and cries and stabbing sharp breaths that had come from Adrian's room that night when Anne-Marie was there, and I awoke with a start in a cold sweat.

I read and I read, and the *Handbook* said that when a Christian soul tried to speak in tongues for the first time and break through to a freer communication with the Lord, Satan was always present, hanging lead weights on his tongue and striving with the Holy Spirit for mastery of his soul. So now, with those guttural words always ringing in my skull, I became afraid even to turn off the light for fear of the presence of Satan who might be in the room; and when I did turn it off I stared hard and fierce into the blackness till it became a sensible, heavy pressure on my eyes and they smarted and hurt because I was afraid even to blink. Everything in the dark room seemed electric, seemed alive with possible sudden movement the moment I relaxed, and Satan was there for certain, I thought, waiting there to strike, and my heart pounded – 'Ravishnah, homorrah homorrah!'

But then in the bright suburban mornings again, all this seemed ridiculous and I set off for school the same as ever, and I did okay in all the sciences and terrible in the arts, and with a couple of friends we cut out the girl on page three of the *Sun* and we used to say, 'Nipples, grade three – Crotch, grade four,' using the same sing-song tone as the man who reads the classified football results on the television. 'Bum, three – Legs, one.' And I never told my friends at school anything about the Holy Spirit or Satan, nothing; just as I would never have confessed to them that at the age I was, I still kept bunny rabbits and had to go and pick spinach and dandelion leaves for them every morning at the bottom of our garden.

A month or so after I heard the sounds from my brother's room, Maggie told Anna that Adrian was having sex with Anne-Marie and that he had sex with lots of other girls too, and Anna went straight off and told Mother; but Mother told Anna not to believe everything Maggie came out with because she had a habit of making up stories, she said, and telling fibs, and this was just a part of the very very big problem that she had.

*   *   *

Father was becoming more and more engrossed in his book which he now wanted to call *A Dove's Wings at the Gates of Hell*. He was particularly involved in explaining why it was often better to speak in another language when we spoke to God, and then why the Lord sent His prophecies in one language through one person and then gave the gift of interpretation to another person so that they could convert them into English. At the heart of this, he considered, could be uncovered the fundamentals of the relationship God wished to cultivate with us in this new Charismatic Age, and the critical difference between what he called prayers (or 'outpourings') of worship, and prayers (or 'supplications') of petition.

So the greater part of his time now Father spent in his study searching though Biblical commentaries with his thick glasses and an orange in his hand, or an apple. He took Morning Song and Evening Song every Sunday as ever, and on Friday he led the Friday Night Worship meeting, which was held in the evening in our lounge and was where everybody really let their hair down and spoke in tongues and sang hymns spontaneously. But most of the other work, and especially the Youth Fellowship, Father left entirely to Rolandson.

Rolandson actually was about thirty-three, and after going to Oxford it seems he had spent a long time working on his uncle's plantation in South Africa until he had been converted there and received his calling, and decided to come back to England and study to be a clergyman. Since she had left Ian, or he her, Anna had started to quite fancy Roley, as she put it, his broad shoulders and crisp blond hair and blue eyes, and now she went to all his prayer meetings and all the Festival of Light rallies he arranged coaches to, and she sat next to him as often as she could and found out all about him.

Apparently, she told me, he had sinned a great deal in South Africa with drink, and perhaps with women too she thought, though he hadn't actually said anything, and that was why as soon as he had been converted he had sworn such a strong vow to strive against sin and all the weaknesses of the flesh so long as he should live. It was a lifelong campaign for him, a crusade almost.

She told me all this with shining eyes, sitting on her bed after we had come back from a Soul-Searching Party, and she said she could really quite fancy being married to Roley with those thick blond bushy eyebrows he had, and I should pray for them that their friendship would grow into love, because she said she felt she could really help Roley because deep deep down he was a sad person. So in my prayers at the end of the day which were becoming ever more mechanical despite how hard I struggled against it, I prayed for my sister to get Rolandson and marry him because I was sorry for Anna: she had acne lately and no breasts at all for all the bras she wore – I knew because I'd seen her naked through the holes somebody had drilled in the bathroom loft-cover to let the steam out – and I thought she might never be able to marry anyone after Ian.

But Rolandson didn't seem at all interested in women. In fact it became a big joke at the Youth Fellowship. There were lots of girls chasing him because he was very handsome and at thirty-three they thought he must be thinking of marrying soon, and also he wasn't poor like most clergymen are because of the shares he had in his uncle's business in South Africa, and he drove a new Rover with twin carburettors. Lots of quite pretty girls chased him, but he showed no interest. He didn't even seem to notice it. And at all the Youth Fellowship meetings he always spoke out very very strongly against sex and against any form of petting between

42

boyfriend and girlfriend – 'Holy Rolandson', we called him. Even kissing, he said, even kissing or any type or form of physical contact whatsoever, laid one wide open to Satan's corrupting hand, so visible in the explosive permissiveness of our time, the mini-skirts and the orgies at rock concerts – and if he ever caught two people necking or even hugging round at the church-hall he used physically to separate them and give them long lectures about setting a good example and sometimes he sent girls home if he thought they were dressed provocatively.

I was sort of half going out with my very first girlfriend at this time and I remember after one of Rolandson's talks we found we had to discuss our friendship very seriously together in the drizzle at her bus-stop outside Owen Owen's, and we decided there was lust in both our hearts and Satan was at work and we should stop seeing each other immediately. I was miserable about it but I had to agree and so when the bus came we pecked each other a puritan goodbye with wet faces from rain and tears together, like old people in films when one of them is going to die; and that night in bed I thought of her: her name was Ruth, Ruth! I thought of her body and I thought of those sounds I had heard on the microphone from Adrian's room and I half wished I'd recorded them on the tape-recorder.

If you look back at this now, the Youth Fellowship and Rolandson's talks and so on, it seems my father could have known nothing of this aspect of his character, I mean of the fanaticism with which he spoke out against sex and the violent anger with which he forcibly separated couples in the dark corridor that ran behind the stage of the church-hall, or again the way he spoke of Satan creeping through the very pores of our sinful flesh. Because if he had known about it, my father, surely he would have understood, absorbed as he was, and found some way to defuse the frenzy that was slowly, ever so slowly building up, and would climax so terribly. But my father trusted implicitly in Rolandson, I think perhaps because Rolandson had been to Oxford which was where *he* had always wanted to go himself and where he had wanted Adrian to go, and where he would have wanted me to go, I suppose, if I wasn't such a borderline case. And then he was even rather pleased, I think, that Rolandson showed no signs of marrying, because my father hated the sort of gossip that surrounded a courting curate, and so he simply buried himself deeper and deeper in that book he was writing, *A Dove's Wings at the Gates of Hell*, or simply *Fire in Our Fingertips*, as he was thinking of calling it now, or *The Burning Bush*.

★   ★   ★

So Anna was not successful with Rolandson, who would treat her only as a friend – 'an ally in Christ', he used to say – and she became very depressed. She was depressed about Rolandson and not getting married or going to China, and she was depressed about her life in general, because she had done badly at school and the world seemed to offer no openings for her, and she felt that my parents, and particularly my father, despised her for this because they had done so well at school and university too and my father was writing another learned book (he had already written one some years ago called *The Sacraments Through 20 Centuries*, which the Scripture Union Press had published, though they didn't pay him for it).

Trying to please, Anna said things like: 'If I had been as clever as that brother of mine, I would never have thrown

it all away on stupid sculpture and modern music. I would
have gone to university and done a PhD', because Father's
passion was that one of us should do a PhD one day.

'I wouldn't have buried my talent in the ground,' she
said grimly, but my father only grunted because he didn't
like to be reminded of Adrian squandering his life studying
modern music, and Mother said 'Shush, love', when Anna
started like this because at any moment she might burst into
tears. Mother said, 'All things work together for good, my
dear, for those who love Christ'; and she said, 'Adrian's just
growing up, bless his dear heart, these are difficult times' –
because my mother liked to see everything bad as 'just a
phase', or 'difficult times', and she didn't like to think that
anything in our family could ever really come to a head in
bloodshed and tears and be permanent and stamped on us for
always.

'Roley would never let him get away with it,' Anna said
to me. 'Roley is a real man. He thinks it's really disgusting
the way Adrian carries on. It's a yoke round Father's neck,
he says.'

Anna involved herself more and more in the church and
she went to every conceivable meeting, with or without
Rolandson, and sang on her guitar 'Raised on a Dove's
Wings', and 'And Should It Be', which was now the most
popular hymn, I think because it had that line, 'My chains
fell off, my eyes could see', which came at the crescendo of
the melody and everybody would raise their arms and sway
from side to side with tears in their eyes it was so moving.
Also she sang a song she had written herself called 'I Am Persuaded My Lord Will See Me Through', which had a very
sad tune, something like 'Home, Home on the Range', in
parts. She used to make my father sing it with her after cocoa
when he stood beside her at the piano.

She went to every conceivable meeting and spoke in tongues everywhere and interpreted prophecies which other people gave in tongues and these prophecies spoke of 'the Latter Days, the last wild throes of Satan', and of 'making ourselves ready for the Lord's Coming'. She was thinking of training to be a Lady Worker, she said, a woman who helps the clergy in big city parishes.

But when there were no meetings and no Soul-Searching Parties to go on, Anna had nothing to do but sprawl on the couch and watch television, because all her life was in the church; and some evenings she watched every programme from seven right until shut-down and while she watched she ate those Fig-Roll biscuits, or Lincoln Tea biscuits, or the éclairs she made Friday night and put in the fridge for the rest of the week, and the sugar just brought her spots out without ever putting an inch on her breasts; so that after the first couple of times I never even went up into the loft any more to look at her when she took a bath.

Adrian came in at ten-thirty or eleven perhaps, after my parents were already in bed. He came into the dining-room in his Afghan coat with a hand-rolled cigarette between his lips and his blond hair held back with elastic bands in a scruffy pony-tail.

'You're not supposed to smoke down here,' Anna said.

He said nothing, Adrian. He sat cross-legged with his club foot on the floor and put the ash from his cigarette into his coat pocket.

'You're disgusting,' Anna said.

She said, 'I wouldn't be surprised if you were on drugs.'

'Face-ache,' he said calmly, and he had his small cynical smile on his face around clenched teeth with his jaw pushed out. He was growing a little goaty beard.

Then at this hour Adrian always wanted to watch some

arts programme on the BBC about modern culture or sub-culture or something, but Anna would already be in the middle of a gangster film or a western with John Wayne and she refused to turn over because the programmes on culture bored her.

So Adrian made dirty, nasty comments on the film.

'Nice pair she's got, don't you think?'

'Nice little bum she's got. Bet she doesn't have any trouble getting laid.'

'You're disgusting,' Anna said. 'Foul.'

'Jealousy won't get you anywhere,' he laughed.

She was furious. She spoke through her teeth. 'I'm not jealous of you, you miserable creature, and I never will be, because I shan't be going where you're going after I'm dead. Because you're going to Hell, that's what!'

Then Adrian would go and change the channel over to the BBC and they would have a flaming row about it. Anna was like my father in a row, she got furious with Adrian's cynical smile, and frustrated, and so she hit at him and it came to blows. Adrian would tease her with little digs, hopping about on his one good foot, hissing and pretending to be demonic, and she would take great swipes at him and even throw the biscuit-box so that it exploded in crumbs on the floor and he roared with laughter. Then my father came storming downstairs in his dressing-gown and if necessary he waded in with blows as well, and he always gave the benefit of the doubt to my sister. 'I don't quite know who you think you are these days,' he said. 'You've grown a mite too big for your boots you have.' And he said, 'The arrogance of you young people these days, it's stupefying!'

Adrian stomped out, slamming the door, and when he was a safe distance he shouted 'Temper, temper', in a sing-song voice and he whistled very loud the tune to 'Raised on a

Dove's Wings', because the words in the third line were, 'Lo, He bringeth peace and love', and then he laughed again banging away up the stairs. 'Goodnight all!'

'It's positively demonic the way he laughs sometimes,' Anna said. She was weeping. 'Like he wasn't my brother at all but somebody else.'

My father went upstairs and prayed for Adrian in tongues with my mother while Anna sniffled in front of her western and the dog gobbled up the biscuits crushed on the floor.

If Maggie was in the dining-room when Adrian came in and argued with Anna she didn't support either side, but stayed perfectly still in her chair right through all of it, not smiling or frowning, but blank with her small brown eyes in her big round face turned away from them to the television perhaps or to her feet. But when it was over and she was still there with Anna alone she would suddenly become very matey; and if Anna was crying she would hug her and she agreed that Adrian was disgusting the way he dressed and spoke and she would wipe Anna's tears away from her thin cheeks and sometimes she would even kiss them away very gently.

'Most blokes are downright disgustin' when you add it up,' she said in her East London accent. 'Look at the way that Ian acted, takin' his word back just when it fancied him. They're all pigs in the end of the day, not countin' your dad of course, that's a special case.'

'And Rolandson,' Anna said, blowing her nose; because she still hadn't lost all hope of Rolandson.

Maggie said she didn't know about Rolandson: he was very religious but she didn't know about him because men were impossible to know about really, however religious they were. They were pigs.

'It's just he's a bit hung up about women, I think,' Anna said.

Maggie snorted. 'It's time some of us were a bit more hung up about men,' she said, and she sat there on the couch beside Anna with her arm laid along the backrest round my sister's neck, watching Katharine Hepburn simper over John Wayne while he shot at people.

But then the following evening perhaps, Maggie would tag along with Adrian and his friends to the pub and now she would say nasty things about Anna: that she was lazy and sloppy and out of shape and she would soon have to pull herself together if she joined the police – oh yes – and one night she said that she, Anna, had a photo of Rolandson in his swimming-trunks from when the Youth Fellowship had gone on a day-trip to Clacton – his knee-length swimming-trunks, raving Puritan that he was – and she kept it under her pillow, Maggie said, and masturbated over it with a bar of soap.

Adrian told me about this in great spirits the following day, laughing his laugh, but then I told him what Mother had told Anna with regard to something else provocative Maggie had once said; that one of her problems was making up stories and lying. Still, Adrian said, whether Maggie had made it up or not, it wouldn't surprise him at all Anna doing that. Not at all. And he said, let her. He said, if it cheered her up all well and good. Everybody played with themselves in the end, didn't they? There was nothing to be ashamed of: the only funny thing was why she had to be such a holy-roller and a Bible-basher at the same time, giving him this charismatic crap day in day out about devils and angels and heaven and hell and all that prehistoric stuff. He laughed.

I didn't say anything, but I went into Anna's room the

following night when she was out at Rolandson's prayer meeting and I looked under her pillow and then high and low through the room, but I didn't find any photograph of Rolandson except the ones there were in the parish magazine of course, and he was wearing all his robes in those and had his face set quite grim and apostolic under the great big bushy eyebrows.

The walls of Anna's room were lemon yellow and there was a poster of Johnny Cash in cowboy outfit and another poster showing a steep wooded mountain and a stream that plunged directly down from above. Underneath it said 'In All Thy Ways Acknowledge Him And He Shall Direct Thy Paths'. Also on her door there was one of those Snoopy posters and this one said, 'You don't have to be mad to live here but it helps.'

I went to bed and read my Bible. I read that chapter in the Old Testament about Onan who spilt his seed upon the ground and the thing which he did displeased the Lord, wherefore He slew him. But to tell the truth the Bible was getting more and more difficult for me these days, and I read it and prayed purely mechanically as a duty so that I wouldn't go to hell like Adrian; but I couldn't make head nor tail of it the way I could with my electronics books; and if I tried to pray in tongues there were just those few awful guttural words that came stuttering out of my throat like coughs of phlegm or blood, 'Ravishnah, homorrah homorrah. Ravishnah, homorrah homorrah!', and those words always seemed to make the very darkness around me alive and furious with fear and with Satan. I lay back trembling, the way you do at night sometimes, rigid with fear, watching my dressing-gown on the door for the moment it would turn into a demon and leap, watching the pale lights of the cars outside stretch and flit across the ceiling, the tossing branches of a tree shaking shadows on the wall. I thought of the noises Adrian and Anne-Marie had made together, and of Roland-son who had sinned probably with women in South Africa – with black women, I wondered? With women like the ones you could see in the stacks of *Geographical Magazines* under the stairs with the strange flat pointed breasts – the ones who went down to the sea every morning and squirted their milk into the water? And then I thought about Maggie and what her problem might be and whether I should tell my mother the way she deliberately played one part with my brother and another with my sister. But I wouldn't tell. I knew I wouldn't. I lay in the dark and I was afraid because I wasn't holy like my father and mother, nor bold like my brother, fearless and godless; so that in the end I didn't know what I was really, or what I wanted to be, except that I was nervous and weak and spineless. Thoroughly spineless.

The next week then I learnt how to bug a phone by taping a tiny coil or choke behind the telephone wired up to the mike input of the church tape-recorder that Father let me borrow to tape the Top Twenty from the radio. There was a big background buzz because it wasn't all very well in-sulated, but everything was quite audible. So it was that I recorded a very long call between my mother and a girl who was pregnant, in which Mother said nothing but 'Yes, yes. Yes, yes' the whole way through; and a call from my father to ask why he hadn't received his cheque for ten funerals he'd done more than a month ago; and a call finally from Maggie, in which she spoke to a woman who had a Scottish accent and whom she called 'lovey', and she said it was okay living in our home, really quite okay, only everybody was a bit loony and God-squaddish. Then they arranged to go for a

drink at a new wine-bar somebody was opening in Crouch
End called the Hen and Chickens.

★   ★   ★

It was in February of the following year my mother was
given a prophecy from the Lord which was considered of
great importance in the church and talked about in all the
various prayer meetings quite incessantly. This was after my
brother had spent the whole of Christmas, practically, locked
in his room with Anne-Marie, without ever even introducing
her to my parents, and Mother had discovered a strange pair
of ladies' panti-hose in the wash, too small to belong to my
sister or Maggie or herself. Adrian denied any knowledge of
these panti-hose; he was quite adamant and said they must
belong to Anna or Maggie, but they denied it too and so for
nearly a week Mother went around half in tears saying
nothing to anybody. My father couldn't understand and
after praying with her for hours and hours he wanted her to
go and see a doctor because nobody had told him, of course,
why she was crying. But she wouldn't go.

To me she said one night, 'Richard, do you think I should
be harder on Adrian?'

I couldn't say anything. Her eyes were red with tears and
it put a lump in my throat to see her like this.

She said, 'In the end, you know, I think I owe it to him to
be harder on him. It's my duty.' But she never was. She was
never hard on him at all.

And then she had this prophecy.

It happened at the Friday Night Worship meeting in our
lounge and I was there. I always came to all these meetings
because Ruth came too, the girl I had broken off with after
one of Rolandson's talks; and at least if we couldn't go out

we could still talk to each other here. When everybody bowed their heads and bent their backs in prayer, I put my hands over my face and I could look through my fingers at where her legs came out of her skirt. She wore a green maxi-skirt because they were in fashion then, but with a tiny slit up one side so that I could see her ankles crossed and then just a glimpse of her leg, shapely and slim, and the tiny feet in cherry-red high heels, the same colour almost as the lipstick she wore. But she was very devout, Ruth, and she prayed a lot out loud for her parents and for her friends at school who followed evil ways, and I never got any indication she glimpsed through her fingers to look at me.

The meetings were like this. First everybody sang with Anna playing on the piano – 'And should it be that I should gain / An interest in my Saviour's blood' – to get into the mood, so to speak; then there was a rousing sermon by a visiting preacher, about Christ's Church Militant in the latter days generally; then two or three testimonies from the church folk about the Lord's goodness over the past week, how He had pulled Alan Ingrams from the pit of depression and given him a Word of Comfort about his job, and how He had eased Madge's arthritis; and after each testimony everybody said, 'Ay-*men*, thanks be to God, who cares for His children' – because this is what Joy Kandinsky used to say. Then there was Communion and the silver cup and plate were passed round in muttering and prayer with the small white napkin you had to wipe the cup with after you drank; and finally there was a long period of what was called 'open prayer', when everybody bowed their heads and prayed silently and waited for the Spirit to move somebody to pray, in tongues perhaps, or to sing out loud. Sometimes there were long periods of silence during this part, periods which became tense and embarrassing and a sort of pressure built up amongst everybody there as they waited and waited for somebody else to break the silence. You could hear the ticking and whirring of our cuckoo clock, the sound of the traffic outside, and the dog sometimes would go snuffling from one person's feet to another while they kept their eyes closed. It became really unbearably tense and each person would be wondering inside their heads whether perhaps they oughtn't to break this silence themselves, to pray, to say something, anything at all; but then they found they had nothing to say – or nothing sufficiently important to break a tension like this. What they had to say would have been all right earlier, but now it was too late. And this waiting and tension generated a general feeling of guilt amongst us all I think, and an intense desire for release: so that when finally somebody did pray and it all finished and we sang the last hymn, 'The Joy of The Lord is My Strength', we did so quite wildly, as if after an ordeal, and everybody held up their arms and closed their eyes in ecstasy; and then afterwards there was coffee and biscuits and we all chattered in loud voices, gaily, me standing right next to Ruth and looking down a bit into her cleavage. Because she was the only girl I knew of our age who had a cleavage already.

Mother's prophecy came in the middle of one of these long silences. I was biting my lips I remember and I always had this fearful desire to start speaking out in tongues, out loud, launching myself on just those three words, 'Ravishnah, homorrah homorrah!' – because the *Handbook* said you must share your gift with others and you should start with whatever word the Lord had given you and if you trusted in Him, He would give you the rest. I sat there trembling, the words pulsing in my mind, 'Ravishnah, homorrah homorrah!', ready at any moment to start shouting them out loud: it was the same kind of feeling almost as when you're looking over a cliff and you suddenly feel you want to jump, you *have* to; jump, destroy yourself; and I would be sweating and sweating away – while at the same time, though almost on another planet it seemed, I was also peeping between my fingers at Ruth's legs and the cherry-red high-heels that had ankle straps and a silver buckle.

Mother spoke in tongues first, suddenly and terribly loud. Her voice was sharp and discordant with that babble of words that were not words tumbling so fast from her mouth. And then after a short silence she interpreted the tongue herself.

'Behold the interpretation of the Word of the Lord!' Her voice jerked and panted rather oddly and she seemed terribly agitated. 'Ye have been given great gifts! Yea, the Lord Thy God has poured down His riches upon thee and upon His church. But to what end? Listen, my children, listen with care, for it is the Lord thy God speaketh and verily I say unto you, the Lord thy God is not proud of His church. He is not proud. I gave you great gifts and you have not used them. I gave you the power to bind Satan and yet Satan is free and bold even in the very midst of your company. Pluck out the eye that offends you! Pluck it out, that thou sin not. Use my gifts, oh my children, use them; or they will not remain long amongst you. Do not bury your talents, nor hide your light behind a bushel. For verily I say unto you, unto he that hath shall more be given, but unto he that hath not, yea, even that which he hath shall be taken away from him and he shall be cast into outer darkness and there shall be weeping and gnashing of teeth.'

She finished, shaking, and a general shiver passed across the assembly, like wind on still water; and the dog whined, scratching at the door to be out.

★   ★   ★

55

As the nights got longer through February and March, I stayed out more and more with friends from school and played football on a piece of waste ground near the brook. We played late into the twilight till we could barely see the ball at all and I lived in such different worlds now, at home and at school, that sometimes I actually dreaded the moment I would get back to our house and hear perhaps those moans and tears from behind the peppermint door of our lounge. I stayed out as late as I could, preferring to miss dinner, preferring just to grab what Mother had left for me under the grill and then sneak upstairs to my room and play with my radio. And now I said I had too much physics homework to go out on the nightly Soul-Searching Parties. I wanted to study physics at university, I said, if a borderline case like me could possibly get in there.

One of these nights walking back from football I met Maggie. She stopped in her white Morris Minor with the radio on very loud singing the Beatles and she asked if I wanted to go to the pub. She was very matey.

'I don't feel like going straight back right now,' she said. 'They'll be 'avin' that Monday Night at Eight meeting and I don't feel like it tonight.'

I said I was miles too young to drink in a pub.

'It's not too nippy though,' she said. 'I'll take you somewhere where we can drink outside. 'Aven't you ever been to a pub before?'

I hadn't.

'Well then,' she said, 'you can't go spendin' yer 'ole life without ever going to a pub, can you now?'

I sat outside and Maggie went in and bought pints of beer. There were a group of rockers too who kept taking turns on their motorbikes to roar up to the war memorial and round and back, timing each other, it seemed, and cheering.

'Bloody idjuts,' Maggie said. 'They'd soon have to shape up if they joined the police. I'd see to that.'

'A bit of bloody discipline is what they need,' she said. She pulled out a packet of Embassy cigarettes and smoked and I hadn't known before she smoked. She never smoked at home. I sipped my beer. It didn't taste very nice but it didn't taste very strong either, so I drank it fast to keep the same speed as her.

'Your mother and father are wonderful people,' Maggie said.

I said yes.

She said, 'Really, I feel very close to your mother after all she's done for me. Very close. Healing me like she has. She's the one perfect person I ever met, I think.'

I wanted to ask her what she'd been healed from, but I didn't dare. I sat still nervous. It was an overcast warm night for March, I suppose, and we sat in the half-light thrown from the yellow windows of the pub and watched the rockers race about the war memorial.

'Bloody idjuts,' Maggie said again. 'They should have more respect.'

'And Adrian's a wonderful lad too,' she said. She smiled me a frank friendly smile from her big loose mouth. She wasn't made-up or even feminine-looking at all, but like a tom-girl and she had some spots on her chin. She sat leant forward with her feet wide apart in cord jeans and her heavy breasts sagging over the table.

'You're lucky living in such a happy family,' she said, sucking froth from her lips.

I said I knew. I was grateful. I really was.

'My father, on the other hand, used to beat me. Really, I was the only child and he used to beat me.' She laughed, lighting another cigarette. 'He used to pull down my knickers and slap my bum – and other things – you wouldn't believe it.'

She laughed and went and bought some more beers and while she was gone I went over what she'd said in my mind and I couldn't work it out, not at all really; except that obviously it was all wrong and perhaps to do with her problem, and in the half-dark I tried to pray for her: 'Dear Lord,' I prayed, 'whatever her problem is, please help her' – only my praying was hopeless these days. It just didn't work.

She said cheerfully, coming back, 'Most men are filthy pigs though.'

'Yes,' I said.

'Have you ever thought for example that for all the way they talk about religion, your mum and dad, they still get between the sheets and do it.'

'Even Holy Rolandson sometimes, I bet.' She laughed.

I hid in the beer, drinking.

'I bet the Lord tells him when to. I bet the Lord tells him when to go to the john and what kind of rubbers to use.' She grinned, draining her beer very quickly, but then she said absolutely straight-faced, 'They've all been very good to me though, healing me like they have, especially your mother.'

'Yes,' I said.

'And Adrian going to bed with Anne-Marie! Leaving her panties in the wash!' She burst out laughing. 'He's a little filthy pig like the rest in the end.'

I had a fit of hiccups.

In the middle of our third beer, she said, 'Ruth's a nice girl, isn't she?' She watched me, smiling across the table. 'Big breasts for a girl her age.' She stubbed out her cigarette into an ashtray that was just an old jar lid.

'Bigger than Anne-Marie's already,' she said.

I said yes. 'She's a year older than me,' I said. My head was swimming with beer and the roar of those motorbikes thundering between my ears.

She said, 'Have you been to bed with her yet?' and she leaned quickly across the table and gripped my wrist so that her fingernails dug right in a moment and hurt. 'Have you?' she said.

At home I was sick. I banged and stumbled through the front door and Maggie had already disappeared somehow. The air was full of women's voices chit-chatter-chattering from the lounge and there was a thick smell of coffee and cakes.

I threw up on the parquet-flooring.

Assistant treasurer of the Mother's Union, Mrs Boycott-Browne, came out of the kitchen with a tray full of crockery.

'Oh, Mrs Bowen!' she cried. 'Your poor boy!'

My head was exploding, but darkly, and swirling and swirling. I swayed over the polished floor looking for my feet. Then two or three soft dresses rustled about me, a thick perfume, strong as gas it seemed, jumped into my throat and I was half heaved, half guided up the broad wide stairs; and while at first there had been that babble-babble of voices, now there was only a hush pressed full of whispers, and through this mist of sound all I could really hear clearly in my head was Maggie's sharp cockney voice – 'Have you? Have you?' – and the drunken cells in my brain were stumbling incoherently from one explanation and answer to another, 'There's no place we can be alone . . . we're not sure we're in love . . . she doesn't think it's time yet – only fifteen . . . Ravishnah, homorrah homorrah!' – and it wasn't clear in my mind whether I was more embarrassed I hadn't been to bed with her, like I was embarrassed about never having been to a pub before, or guilty that I wanted to, I was aching to, aching; and really I wasn't sure what I was trying to explain to whoever I was talking to, or what they wanted to hear through that mist of pressed hushed whispers, which finally swallowed me up, I suppose, consciousness and all, somewhere around the top of the stairs.

Mother contrived not to let Father hear about my being sick. When I woke up in the morning she was sitting by my bed biting her bottom lip.

'Who gave you alcohol to drink?' she said.

My head was thumping and my lips and eyes were dry.

'Who got you drunk? Who were you with yesterday evening?'

I said friends. She said I wasn't old enough to drink, how on earth had I managed to get hold of drink with my friends? I looked about in my mind, banging and throbbing and dry.

'Home brew,' I said. 'One of them made it himself from a Boots packet. We didn't realize how strong it was.'

Then Mother began to weep with her head bent low over me on the bed and she said it would drive her to an early grave, it really would, if I followed the same evil course my brother had – it would be the death of her, quite absolutely the death. She was already worn to a frazzle and more just with the worry and her hair was going grey and she couldn't honestly see quite what she'd done to deserve it.

I said no.

Even Maggie, she said, still crying, who had had such a hard childhood and so many problems, even she set a better example than we boys did.

Drink was evil, she said.

'I forbid you to drink,' she said. 'You'll bring me down with grey hairs to my grave.'

I wanted to be hard with my mother the way Adrian was, the way he could set his face quite pitiless and hard and

60

triumphant – but then at the sight of her red eyes and the distress she felt, I started crying too and I said I'd never never do it again, never – it was just a mistake we'd made, not understanding how strong the beer was. Really, perhaps my friend hadn't followed the instructions right when he made it or something. But I'd never drink alcohol again, I promised.

So then when I'd finally worked myself up into a state like this so that I was almost sobbing with guilt, she took advantage of it by insisting I go out that minute and have my hair cut. She wasn't going to have me going round like a lout like my brother did, with my hair smothering my shoulders, she said. I should look smart if I wanted to get on in the world. Otherwise I'd be the death of them all. So I had to get up and to go out and have my hair cut right away, even with that throbbing headache.

When Adrian saw me in the evening he burst out laughing. 'I told Father we should have had the lawnmower adjusted,' he said and he said, 'Maggie told me all about it. She said you drank like a little fish.'

I kept looking out of the window in my room. I had to look away because my eyes were watering. He came and took my arm, still laughing. 'Hey, don't let it get to you though Ricky! Life is for fun. Want a game of Risk?'

But I didn't want to play Risk any more with Adrian – because wherever there was a dice involved he always won. Always. Adrian always won everything. He was so strong. He never had to have his hair cut, never, and he'd been going to bed with his girlfriend for more than a year.

★   ★   ★

As I said, Mother's prophecy caused quite a stir in the church and my Father slowed down the writing of his book a bit which was called *Spiritual Warfare* now, and he arranged some more meetings and spoke at a lot of weekend conferences which the Festival of Light and a new organization called the Fountain Trust used to arrange in order to 'introduce you to the Holy Spirit', as they put it in their brochure. Sometimes he and Mother and Anna and Maggie all went away for the whole weekend to these conferences and then Adrian had Anne-Marie over and she stayed the night. Adrian even went downstairs sometimes and made tea and brought it to her in bed. I know because I heard him limp past my door with the tray rattling.

But the real problem, everybody agreed, was how to come to grips with Satan himself: how to grapple with him and throttle him and use the gifts that the Most High had given – everybody was convinced of it now – expressly for this purpose. And it was here that Rolandson showed himself the most zealous and enterprising.

There was in the city at that time a great deal of interest in black magic and there were a number of films going around which used the subject as background for thrillers and for pornography too. So having burnt everybody's Black Widow and Black Sabbath records, and having almost obliterated any physical signs of affection in the Youth Fellowship, Rolandson turned his sights to these; and he wasn't content with concentrating on the Gaumont that was in our parish, because generally they only showed one bad film a month and all the rest was Disney; plus, he couldn't really go and picket the two other Odeons in the suburb, because then the clergymen who controlled those parishes would say he was treading on their toes. So instead he started going down to the city proper and the city now he began to refer to as 'Gomorrah'.

'Satan reeks through the pores of the fleshpots of Gomorrah!' he began sharply from the pulpit. 'You will forgive me if the words seem somewhat antiquated, brethren, but we must call things by their names. So let us be clear, once and for all, that what we are talking about is vice, is sin, is corruption and death.' He stopped, half-frowning, half-smiling from under his bushy eyebrows. 'And Lot said unto the Lord,' he suddenly thundered, taking the congregation by surprise, '"Lord," he said, "Lord, oh Lord! Let me but find a hundred, a hundred godly men in the city, and wilt Thou spare it? Wilt Thou?" And the Lord in all His mercy said He would.' Rolandson paused. He said quietly, 'Never let us forget it is a merciful God we have, my friends, ay-men, a merciful God.' And then he suddenly shouted again – that was his trick, to be quiet and tender and then suddenly to shout – 'But in all the city of Gomorrah, yea in all the city of Gomorrah, Lot could not find a hundred good men, nay, amid the brothels and casinos and the dens of vice and corruption, he could not find fifty, he could not find ten. And the Lord's wrath was kindled against that unholy place and He said . . .'

In the back row I writhed my fingers together, sweating, and I wore a polo-neck collar to try and hide how badly the barber had cut my hair at the back. I felt almost sick in the church these days, as if I was really physically ill, and those words would come back and back and back to my mind, 'Ravishnah, homorrah homorrah!' My mother though was totally behind Rolandson now and she nodded her head constantly and said, 'Ah-men.' It was the only vestige of her old resistance that she never got into the habit of saying 'Ay-men' like the others.

So now instead of the old Soul-Searching Parties in the High Road, Rolandson loaded perhaps six or seven people into his Rover with the twin carburettors and they went down into the city, to Soho perhaps, or to any cinema that was showing a Satanic or pornographic film, or to a theatre where there was nudity on stage maybe, and then they knelt and prayed right on the pavement outside for the poor damned souls within and Anna played her guitar and sang 'Raised on a Dove's Wings', and they handed out tracts to the people going in and coming out of the show.

Hence it was one evening Adrian came out of a cinema in Hampstead where they had been showing a film by Ken Russell and he walked straight into Rolandson preaching under a black umbrella. He was in full swing, the clergyman, in his long black cassock, damp blond hair and eyes flashing in the phosphor yellow light of the street, and he waded in straight away.

'Aren't you ashamed of yourself, Adrian Bowen? You who have been brought up in the very bosom of Christ, who should be as a banner to the righteous!'

Anne-Marie said, 'Who's he?'

Anna told me later she thought she'd seen Maggie tagging along behind Anne-Marie, but if this was true then she must have disappeared at once. Anna it seems was stood there singing 'I am persuaded the Lord will see me through', with four or five others who were handing out tracts.

Adrian said he was in a hurry and tried to push by.

'Young man!' Rolandson thundered. 'I am talking to you in the name of Christ. You are a yoke around your father's neck. You are knocking on the very gates of Hell!'

'Who *is* he?' Anne-Marie said.

'Inviting eternal perdition!'

Adrian turned and faced Rolandson. He pushed out his goaty beard and found the little cynical smile with a rolled cigarette still glued to one of his lips.

'Somebody,' he replied quite loud to Anne-Marie, 'who

64

has a small bloody fortune invested in South Africa. That's who he is.' He turned to Rolandson. 'Has your money killed any blacks today?'

And in the brief moment then that Rolandson was silenced, Adrian turned and went, pulling the tiny Anne-Marie behind him, hatless and coatless both, in the clothes they bought from Oxfam shops and wearing those high-ankle plimsolls you used to buy from Woolworth's, called Bumper boots. The light washed about them on the wet pavements, Adrian disappearing with his furious stumbling determined walk.

★   ★   ★

This was early March and it was all to come to a climax of course at the houseparty in April. But first, Rolandson did a brave, an almost astonishing thing. He sold all the shares he had in his uncle's business and gave all the money away to Christian Aid. According to Anna it came to twenty-five thousand pounds. He buttonholed Adrian then at the bus-stop outside the church door.

'You showed me where Satan was hidden in my heart,' he said.

'Not precisely my intention,' Adrian said, and he'd begun to speak in the dry flat voice the Beatles used in their films these days. Also he wore sunglasses even when it wasn't sunny.

'Everything to Christian Aid,' Rolandson said.

'Everything!' he insisted.

'Fair enough then. Now you're like the rest of us.'

'Ay-men,' Rolandson said fervently, and they stood together on the patch of grass outside the church, Roland-son's cassock lifting and falling with the wind and my

65

brother's hair likewise, excepting that one blond strand he chewed continually in his mouth.

'And you don't feel moved to make a similar sacrifice?'

' 'Fraid I don't have the dough in the first place, mate.'

'But it's your heart the Lord wants, not your money.'

Adrian said, 'How very carnivorous,' in the way probably he thought John Lennon would. He tried to move but Rolandson put a hand on his shoulder.

'Adrian, Adrian,' he said, 'you were the Lord's instrument in prompting me to give away this money and I made this sacrifice praying, even begging the Lord that he would liberate your soul in return. We want to save you.'

But the funny thing was how Adrian knew the Bible and Christianity as well as any clergyman, being brought up the way we were and having the mind he had. 'How does it go?' he said, smiling, ' "Therefore when thou doest thine alms, do not sound a trumpet before thee as the hypocrites do in the synagogue that they may have the glory of men. But give in secret that the Lord which seeth in secret may bless thee openly." '

Then he said, 'Sorry, Donald, but that's my bus. Got to shift my arse, if you'll excuse the expression. Got to be abroad in the world with all the other evil spirits.' He hissed and moved his fingers in that, 'I'm–casting–a–spell way' he had picked up, laughing gaily.

So Rolandson was put down for the second time and my brother hobbled off to catch the bus to Gomorrah.

'Why does he have to bug me so much?' Adrian asked me later.

I was watching out of the window with my binoculars. It was twilight when people came home and went to their bedrooms and changed without drawing the curtains and then went back to their sitting-rooms to turn on the television.

'Why does he have to make such a dick of himself like that?'

I shrugged my shoulders. There was a man in a string vest lighting a cigarette standing by his window.

'I never asked him to give away his stupid money. I don't have to feel guilty about it.'

And he said, 'God, Ricky, for Christ's sake, you're a secretive little bastard you are, never saying a word to anyone but staring into everybody else's business all the bloody time! Whose side are you on in the end, theirs or mine?'

There was a chorus in church that said 'Are you on the Lord's side?', and it always turned my stomach inside every time we sang it. But now I felt just as guilty with Adrian as I did at church. I was guilty not to be on their side and guilty not to be on his. And I myself didn't have a 'side' at all. I was neutral, nothing. The man over the road scratched his stomach under his vest.

Adrian laughed. 'By the way, I know all about you going up into the attic to look through the holes in the bathroom cover.'

I turned at last. I was horrified. How did he know? 'Adrian!' But he was already stomping out of the room.

'Don't know why you bother,' he shouted, 'the women there are in this house, not a tit worth tuppence between them,' and he went into his room and put on a new Rolling Stones record he'd bought. 'Let's Spend the Night Together', with the volume very loud.

A week later my mother went into his room while he was at college and she took away this record and 'confiscated' it, as she put it, because it was disgusting. Adrian discovered the bits in the bin. He said, 'Leave a note for me when the

Grand Inquisitor arrives, I'd like to make sure I have my black cat with me,' and he went out banging the front door.

Anna said, 'That brother of mine. Sometimes! You should have heard how rude he was to Roley,' and my mother and father exchanged glances. Father didn't play chess with Adrian any more because what with all the extra meetings he was taking and this book he was trying to write, he didn't have time.

Maggie was there in the kitchen when they had this argument. In her very strong accent she said, 'It in't nothin' to worry yerself about, Mrs Bowen. He's just at that age,' – which made my mother smile very kindly at her. She thought the world of Maggie. I think she thought she was a great success and a peacemaker, because she was friends with Anna and with Adrian both at the same time.

The following week walking home from football I saw Maggie sitting at a table outside the Keg and Glass and the person she was with, oddly enough, was Anne-Marie. I didn't say hello to them. I ducked down Rose Crescent and watched them from a distance Then they got up quite suddenly and went and climbed into Maggie's Morris Minor. I thought of that phone call I'd heard when she called her friend 'lovey' and said everybody in our house was a bit God-squaddish, but I couldn't make head nor tail of it all.

It was about that time too that I learnt how to cross from our attic to Rolandson's through a small dark tunnel, the two houses having been originally built as one. But there were no holes drilled in the attic covers here like there were in our house. I just heard Rolandson whistling 'The Wise Man Built His House upon the Rock', over the sound of the radio.

Dinner was late again that night because Mother was

speaking in tongues to a girl who was weeping behind the peppermint doors of our lounge. Father watched the news on TV with Adrian who grinned constantly over his shoulder at me and said:

'My word, what's all that racket?'

'My word, it is unpleasant.'

PART TWO

The House Party

The Youth Fellowship houseparty was arranged for Easter time – as always – and, as always, it was to be held at Copplesford, a massive rambling old boarding school situated on the hills south of the city. Each day at Copplesford the following programme prevailed: breakfast at eight, morning meeting at nine; then, ten-thirty till lunch, recreation of any and every kind; lunch till supper, coach trips, prayer meetings, recreation – as one chose; after supper, a long long long meeting, then a further half-hour of recreation, then cocoa, then evening prayer and discussion in the dormitory, then sleep. In short, food, religion and recreation, turn and turn and turn about.

The idea behind the thing was that all the faithful of the Youth Fellowship, some sixty strong, should come, bringing with them if possible some of their unfaithful friends, perhaps ten or twenty; then, with the leaders of the church preaching and so on every morning and night, by the end of the week the unfaithful would all have become faithful. Generally this worked, if for no other reason than because of peer pressure, coupled with that immense emotional turmoil you experienced anyway in your teens at the beginning of spring – especially city youngsters out in the country – and coupled too with the guilt you tended to feel at having the opposite sex around you all the time and lusting the way you would and being forever embarrassed and insecure because of the suspicion you had that you were making a fool of yourself and everybody else thought you stupid, having a haircut like you did or a broken nose or a behind that stuck out. So everybody was converted in the end or they had their faith renewed and everybody played and prayed and sang with all their energy and invented emotional problems and solved them with tears and joy – then at the end of the week they went back home and everything returned to normal. Some of the faithful would become unfaithful and some of the unfaithful who had become faithful would remain so, and the numbers were always about the same. The houseparty proved no more than a kind of powerful emotional and spiritual pressure cooker that seemed terrifically momentous while it happened but then drifted back in the memory to just another holiday.

Only this year of course there was the Holy Spirit to contend with.

And Rolandson.

Plus, in the ears of all the elders of our suburban church were ringing the words of my mother's prophecy, 'The Lord thy God is not proud of His church – for Satan is free and bold even in the midst of your company.'

And there was Maggie.

Adrian had been to the houseparty every year previously and taken part in it just like everybody else. But he hadn't come to church for nearly a year now – he hadn't even come at Christmas, having Anne-Marie in his room like he did – and so this time he said he didn't want to come to the house-party; there was no point in it, he said, because he didn't believe in God at all any more, he really and honestly didn't, and he didn't want to have to listen to endless people trying to persuade him to the contrary.

So he had said it at last, out loud – he didn't believe in God – and I remember how extraordinary and disturbing it seemed at the time that there should be somebody in our house who didn't believe in God, at all, and who could say it. It was as if the place trembled slightly and shook.

And he wouldn't go to the houseparty, he said.

He had to come, Father said.

Mother bit her lip, knitting in the dining-room with the dog snuffling at her feet. Tears pricked her eyes.

Because otherwise, my father said, what proof was there he wouldn't go and smoke drugs right here in the vicarage and the police would catch him and there would be a scandal to end all scandals?

'Ah, so it isn't a free country after all. I might as well be in Russia in the end if . . .'

'Rubbish!' Father thundered. 'Downright, unadulterated rubbish! I won't have you twist the truth like that.'

Mother counted her stitches with clenched teeth, working her lips. Adrian didn't believe in God. He was going to Hell.

'It's not a free country for minors known to have delin-quent tendencies,' Father shouted. 'When you reach your majority you can go to perdition any way you choose, but until then you'll please to obey me, my laddie – and without distorting my words thank you very much.'

Adrian said very seriously, almost gently, 'Father, I promise, I offer you my word of honour, I won't . . .'

But he had made the mistake of getting Father in a temper already. And once Father was in a temper and had taken a position, he would never back down from it; that was the kind of person he was, he would never never back down, however much, later, he probably yearned and wished and longed and longed that he had let Adrian stay at home. Because my father loved Adrian more than any of us, I imagine. He loved Adrian's strength and manliness.

'My word of honour,' Adrian said. 'Please.'

'I don't feel inclined to accept it,' Father snapped, and Adrian stamped out of the room, slamming the study door.

A moment later Father came into the dining-room and stood by Mother where she was knitting. He picked up an orange and tore the skin off it fiercely so it split open and stickied his hands and shirt.

'Stupefying!' he said. His black hair was standing on end.

'Perhaps we haven't been hard enough on the boy.' Mother spoke through bitten lips.

'No, it's my fault,' Father said. He had his mouth full of orange. 'My fault for letting myself get worked up like this. I always get worked up with the boy.'

I was ashamed of my father sometimes, the way he ate. His chin was dribbling and his fingernails were full of pith. I shrivelled with embarrassment when we had guests and if ever he suggested going out to a café or a restaurant as a special treat, I used to refuse.

So the houseparty got off to something of a bad start as far as our family was concerned. Adrian did, however, manage to work out a tacit agreement with my father that even if he had to go he wouldn't actually have to attend the meetings. Even a minor should have religious freedom, he said, especially if he was denied freedom of movement. My father only grunted, trying not to get worked up.

So Adrian told Anne-Marie he was going on the house-party and then she wanted to go too. He didn't want her to go because he was embarrassed, I suppose, about his family and how much religion there would be and so on, but the more he tried to dissuade her, the more she insisted on going. Probably she thought it was a move to give her the brush, as it were – perhaps Maggie even hinted at that in the middle of saying that all men were pigs, one time. But anyway Anne-Marie was determined to go – and so she paid her money and went and of course they put her in the same dormitory with my sister and Maggie. Because she was a prime target.

★   ★   ★

'We are not here in retreat,' Rolandson said. 'We are here to arm ourselves for the greatest advance the world has ever known. For these are the Latter Days.'

This was the second night in the musty assembly hall of the boarding school. To one side was a great sheet of glass running with rain. A french window gave on to a paved terrace and below, a stretch of green sloped soft and soggy to the darkness of a pine wood: smoking beyond that was the village of Copplesford. Then, as Rolandson launched into his first sermon of the week on the theme of the Second Coming and the Chosen and the Lost, two figures picked their way across this muddy patch, just visible in the twilight, Adrian and Anne-Marie, arm in arm and kissing occasionally. They disappeared into the wood and everybody knew of course there was only one possible place they could be going to in the village – to the pub, the evil of drink. Rolandson stopped still and simply watched them a moment, that great Roman brow of his knitted above the bushy eyebrows; then continued.

Afterwards, I sat with Ruth and played draughts. We must have been the only quiet ones in the place and from the tuck-shop where cocoa was served there was the sound of my sister strumming 'Thou Art Worthy', and Maggie trying to rouse some of the girls to a pillow fight. I said to Ruth, did she want to go out for a little walk, surely it couldn't be wrong to go out and walk and talk together. I was all worked up after sitting there still on a wooden chair so long, twisting my fingers in sweaty knots and arguing and arguing inside myself about what Rolandson had said about the Antichrist and Armageddon.

Ruth had on a wet-look white blouse and you could see her bra through it. Her necklace was fake pearls that made her skin look creamy and it sharpened the deftness of her lip-stick somehow – the creaminess and then that sharp sharp redness, with polished teeth between.

I said, just a short walk.

It was raining, she said, and she played the game of draughts very seriously, without once looking up at me, wrinkling the skin over her nose. She wiped me off the board to tell the truth. It was a way she had with her kings I couldn't get on top of at all. Then she said she had to go and prepare a talk for tonight's dormitory session, and she went.

I prowled. I prowled and prowled around. Going past the counselling room I heard a fierce whispering and weeping, a low rhythmical murmur and it seems two souls were brought to Jesus that evening. In fact my mother said later that one of the girlies had been blessed with the most beautiful 'tongue' she had ever heard. Mother always called a girl a 'girly' after she had been brought to the Lord.

Adrian came in very very late, long after the dormitory discussion which was on Galatians 4:12, and he smelt of drink. I listened in the close dark as he picked and stumbled between the beds chuckling to himself, but nobody seemed to wake up, or if they did they didn't want to say anything. I wondered if he came in so late because he didn't want everybody to watch him undress and see the twisted foot, how ugly and wrong it was – or if he did it for the hell of it, or both. But either way, the next night he took four other people down to the pub with him, because it was typical of Adrian that he wasn't satisfied with skipping the meetings on his own. He had to convert people to his own way of thinking; he was like Father in that, always engaged in a polemic, whereas I was like my mother, I suppose; I wanted everybody to be quiet.

He took Mick Potter, whom he knew from college, and Mick's friend, Sandy, then a boy called Andy with his girlfriend, Denise, because they wanted to get out a while to smooch, they said, away from you-know-who. And so the next morning the leaders of the houseparty, my mother and father and Rolandson and a young sidesman called Nigel Matthews, were all in terrific consternation because on the slope of dewy green beyond the french window that morning Maggie had found an empty piece of silver foil with the name Durex stamped on it – and she'd taken it directly to where the elders were praying together before breakfast, because she thought it was her duty to let them know, she said. She smiled and left.

Rolandson wanted to announce the discovery at once and prise the culprit out into the open. The stink of corruption was too strong, he said. But my father said a mere piece of foil paper like that could have been there for weeks, there was no certainty at all that it had been one of the Fellowship – it could even have blown there from miles away. And anyway, he said, the church should never allow itself to become like the Catholic Church had been with its witch hunts and

Spanish Inquisitions. They were there to preach the gospel and nothing else and in the end if certain people wanted to sin they were at more than liberty to do so. It was a free world, my father said, and you couldn't compel people to salvation.

Rolandson was silent, burning; Matthews simply embarrassed, and my mother silent too with bowed heavy head, because she was convinced of course it was Adrian had used what was inside that tin foil to do what for some reason she always feared most for her children and seemed to feel almost guilty of herself.

'And who knows,' my father suddenly went on in a very rare diversion from orthodoxy, 'who knows but that from a young and furtive love might spring a stable, a fruitful Christian marriage?' Who could say, he said, or had the right to judge what was in their youthful minds in these difficult times?

'Bless their dear dear souls,' Mother said carefully, almost blushing, with all the while that guilty scrap of tin foil shouting from the table before them that Maggie had found apparently on the green-sward at pretty well the crack of dawn.

'Ay-men,' Matthews mumbled, scratching the corner of his mouth.

But Rolandson snorted. He snorted fiercely and he muttered to himself something about Satan, and I suppose that was the first time he and my father realized they didn't see eye to eye over this, only neither of them wanted to admit it, even to themselves perhaps. Then afterwards, Rolandson went directly to sit next to my sister at breakfast and he talked to her in low tones; because they were more than ever allies in Christ, Rolandson and my sister now. And he said it was just possible that Father was letting his view of the world be distorted because Adrian was his son and this was extremely dangerous, he said.

★   ★   ★

It rained all week, thick drizzle from a blank sky, sifting on to heavy clay, a weary sad rain, puffed about now and then by a damp wind. A typical English spring it was, I suppose, the earth half awake but struggling to go back to sleep again, pulling the thick grey blanket of the cloud over its head, and rain and rain and more rain. So it was that apart from the occasional muddy sally down to the football pitch, we were all of us locked and bolted in that boarding school as if it was a prison. We were trapped in the great still rooms which had an atmosphere of awkwardness about them, something to do with the empty sound of your feet on bare floorboards and that feel of being in someone else's territory out of season. The windows, looking out on all that dullness, were so dull themselves they might have been bricked up, and on your own in a corridor perhaps, or fetching a pen from your dormitory, you caught yourself glancing over your shoulder for someone in the creaking silence there – for a movement your eye had imagined, furtive in the stale shadows, a devil or a ghost – the world for us had been made so alive, so thick with spirits.

There was no television in the place and only one gramophone, in the tuckshop, where they played records by Merv and Madge Danvers who sang spiritual songs at Fountain Trust Festivals. There was a snooker room and a table-tennis room and a room to play quiet games in and in the assembly hall when there wasn't a meeting you could play your guitar if you had one. My sister was there teaching people how to do American country fingerpicking, which Adrian despised.

Or if you wanted to talk about God or be Baptized in the Holy Spirit you could go to the counselling room where there was always my father or my mother or Donald Rolandson or Nigel Matthews or one of the dormitory leaders, to read to you from the Bible and lay hands on you. In fact there was always somebody there from seven in the morning till midnight.

Our nerves wound up. We were all in love, or at least we all had a crush on somebody, and we were all excited and nervous about sex and excited and nervous about God and about what He thought about our being excited about sex. I remember at the time I was so afraid of sinning in my mind that when I went to bed I always used to imagine I had married Ruth before I would let myself imagine even kissing her. I used to imagine the whole marriage service almost word for word before I would think of her breasts in the bra you could see through the wet-look blouse. And we were all like that, I think. Everybody was afraid of being left out, left out of anything, and some of us were afraid of being too deeply involved, and we all felt guilty, to a man; and anybody who had a personal problem at home, like having no breasts, or having acne, or badly cut hair, then that problem was multiplied a thousand times here in the intensity and press of social contact. So the counselling room beckoned and tugged us like a magnet. We milled and milled and talked and watched each other; watched everywhere for the one we had a crush on, for a moment to be alone, to touch perhaps what it was so strictly forbidden to touch. Right and wrong were magnified to explosives. And all the while, inside its streaming windows, the school smelt of paraffin heaters and instant coffee and sad mashed potatoes, and from the tuckshop wafted the music of Merv and Madge, innocuous as the drizzle, but insistent, 'Surely goodness and mercy shall follow me all the days, all the days of my life' – the beat of the tambourine, '. . . all the days of my li-i-ife . . . surely surely . . .' – while Rolandson roamed the long dusty corridors in his cassock, looking for couples to separate.

People did strange things. On the third night one girl confessed in the open-prayer session of the meeting that there was another girl in her dormitory she wanted to kill, and she dreamt every day of hacking her to pieces with an axe and mixing her up with the food in the kitchen. Off she was whisked to the counselling room. The unbelievers were carefully watched for the moment they would crack and become believers like everybody else, watched eagerly, almost greedily, and one by one they were whittled down. On the third day somebody wrote 'Roley is a Wanker' in red spray paint on the wall by the main door and the next evening one of the unbelievers confessed to it, one who was a bit of a rocker and had sideburns down to his chin and acne. He went into the counselling room with my mother and she came out hours later saying, 'What a nice lad he is now.' He was transformed and had spoken in tongues; and Terry stood behind her, hunched and sheepish in his great leather jacket that had 'Hunt to Kill' written on the back in silver press studs.

Then that night, right in the middle of the night, Maggie got out of her bed and got into bed with my sister and clung to her naked because she said she could feel the Devil in the shape of her father was trying to get back into her and she was terrified. Anna was pleased at first because she always wanted to win Maggie away from Adrian. But when Maggie hugged tighter and tighter and wouldn't be comforted and wanted to bury her head in my sister's neck and below she became afraid too and she woke up the whole rest of the dormitory and made them pray for Maggie and sing choruses. Anne-Marie sat up shivering, hugging the sheets

81

round her – never said a word but only stared. And almost every night in the great assembly hall, Alan Ingrams confessed to deep depression and begged the Lord would set him free. He had been fired from his job, it seemed, the previous week and was drowning in the pit of depression.

I said to Adrian, 'They found a Durex packet on the front green this morning and they're crazy about it.'

'Nothing to do with me.' He laughed. 'Not my brand.'

'What nuts they are!' he said. 'You'd think the world was ending a week on Friday the way they carry on. Want to come to the pub tonight?'

He was quite enjoying himself I think. And I thought it was funny the way he managed to enjoy himself almost wherever he was. I thought perhaps even when he went to Hell, if people really did go there, he would enjoy himself.

'Come on,' he said. 'The beer's remarkably cheap in this part of the world. Fourpence down on London.'

I was too young, I said.

'Be a devil,' he laughed. But I wouldn't.

The only communal thing Adrian joined in was the snooker competition, and he won it of course. He played with a cigarette in his mouth and a hair-band round his forehead, clomping back and forth round the table making cynical intimidating remarks. Anne-Marie sat cross-legged on the huge window-sill watching though the narrow space her long loose hair left, just a sliver of white flesh each side of her Hampstead-thin nose, and then the great dark brown eyes she had, huge and round as the buttons on my mother's Sunday coat. She was silent, watching him, and she was silent really with everybody except Adrian and sometimes Maggie. She never spoke a word, not one tiny word to me. I thought she must despise me.

Adrian played Rolandson in the quarter-final and he said things like, 'Now that's a bloody evil thing to do,' when Rolandson snookered him – 'if you'll 'scuse my French,' he added, pulling on his cigarette. Or he said, 'You demon you, you absolute demon!' if the clergyman got down more than two balls in succession. Rolandson said nothing and played listlessly, indifferently. And even so Adrian only beat him on a final lucky strike with the black. Because when he wanted to, the truth was Roley was quite an ace at snooker, having played day in day out in South Africa. So Anna told me.

In recreation time I went around with Nigel Matthews's younger brother, Alec. We found an entrance to the loft and explored up there without ever saying to each other what we were looking for, but there were no entrances over the girls' bedrooms or bathrooms. There were lots of chests though on the rafters full of the students' things and in one we found a pile of magazines. We leafed through them up there in dust and torchlight, like two criminals looking for unnameable treasure, but there was nothing interesting. Then when we got back to the cover we'd climbed in at and opened it a crack to see if the coast was clear, who should we spy sitting right on the table we'd put there in the corridor to climb down to, but Ruth with Alec's elder brother, Nigel. They were arm in arm, quite tight together, staring out of a drizzly window down to pine woods – and he was ten years older than her if he was a day.

*　　*　　*

The houseparty began Easter Monday and went on for seven days till the Monday of the following week. On Saturday by a miracle Anne-Marie was sort of half-converted, and then on

Sunday my father had to go back home for the day to preach at our church – and thus it was that he gave Rolandson a free rein at the climax of events, to come in for the kill, as it were.

Saturday afternoon, damp and dull as ever, was the afternoon of the snooker finals and for some reason, whether because they had had an argument, or because simply she was fed up of sitting on a cold window-sill watching long games of snooker, Anne-Marie didn't attend. So for the first time, apart from the few moments it took to go to bed in the evening and get oneself up in the morning, Anne-Marie was on her own, away from Adrian – and Anna buttonholed her at once. Anna was in her element at houseparties, always bright and bursting with excitement and even her acne seemed to clear up with burning off so much emotional energy: she was pleasant, bubbly and very earnest.

Did Anne-Marie want to go down to Oxted, shopping, she asked, with Maggie? Everybody else was down there playing Hunt the Spy – a silly game this was, where some people who were supposed to be spies disguised themselves amongst the regular townsfolk and the others had to try and spot them and, when they did, approach them with some ridiculous password, which this year was 'Are your teeth your own?' and the whole fun of the game lay in saying that to the wrong person. But they themselves didn't have to join in, Anna said; they could just go shopping. So Anne-Marie was lulled by all this talk and she said yes, okay, she'd go, and they went down to town in Maggie's car.

Maggie bought a pair of red brushed cord jeans and Anne-Marie found a black handbag she liked in a Help the Aged shop and then they went for a quiet tea in Jolyon's – because she didn't want to run into all the other crowd, Anna said. They sat and ordered tea and cream-cakes and then Maggie noticed a tramp sitting across on the next table. She said suddenly she was sure, positive as positive, he wasn't a tramp; he was one of the spies, because he looked far too young to be a tramp: so she wanted to go over to him and say, 'Are your teeth your own?' But Anna said not to be ridiculous, his beard looked quite genuine, and his teeth even more so – horrible! They all watched the tramp for a minute and Anne-Marie began to giggle.

When Anna pounced.

'Haven't you ever believed in God?' she asked.

Surprisingly, Anne-Marie said she had, in fact, actually she did. 'I just don't see any reason to get so worked up about it,' she said nervously, never taking her eyes off that tramp. And so it turned out she was shy rather than arrogant. She was really quite a nice person.

'But if it's a matter of Heaven or Hell?' Anna insisted, and she began to say how she didn't like to say it but as far as she could see unless something was done about it Adrian was steaming full-speed-ahead to perdition and eternal torture. She sipped her tea. And as people who loved him they owed it to him to struggle to change his mind before it was too late.

Anne-Marie said she couldn't see why God should be so unpleasant as to go sending people to eternal torture. She was timid but quite sure of herself in a way, blinking from behind those tresses of dark Hampstead hair, and she said people had to do all sorts of things to learn from experience and that was why Adrian had taken drugs once, but he wasn't sinful in himself. Maggie put a hand on Anne-Marie's on the red and white check of the Jolyon's tea-table.

Then Anna launched into a full-blown explanation of Heaven and Hell and how it came about that despite a loving God whose very nature was charity, so many people ended up going to the second place because of the demons that

85

possessed them. She was earnest and her eyes shone. No, her weak blue eyes really shone when she spoke like this, because this was her one and only sphere of influence in the end and she loved it so very much. 'If experience is good just for the sake of it,' she said – and now she was repeating the words Father used with Adrian when he came out with this argument – 'then nothing would be wrong, would it? Nothing. You could kill me just for the experience. Because experience,' she finished, 'is just another word for indulgence in the end,' and she smiled quite brilliantly.

Before they left half an hour later, Anna had them all bowing their heads right there at the rickety table in Jolyon's and she prayed out loud for Adrian's twisted soul and thanked God for bringing her and her sister, Anne-Marie, to a greater understanding and to a friendship the one with the other. 'May you give her the power to persuade him to come to the meeting tomorrow night,' she prayed, 'and to forsake his sin and arrogance for Your True Name's Sake, ay-men.'

Maggie said nothing through all of this. She didn't even say all men were disgusting. When Anna prayed she didn't even say ay-men; she had her eyes open watching Anne-Marie. But as they left she turned and winked broadly at the tramp at the table next to theirs, and obviously she had realized that was me.

★   ★   ★

I stayed in the café another ten minutes and then went out into the street. I was afraid the drizzle might upset my make-up, so I hung around under the awnings of shops buying fruit and looking at book titles and magazines in the newsagent's. I had a coat full of holes, trousers too big for me and a grey-brown wig – the same stuff they used on the house-party every year. But nobody recognized me. I was a bit disappointed really; I thought perhaps I was playing the part too well. In an hour and a half only three people asked me were my teeth my own and I gave them one word of the secret message they had to work out by contacting all the spies. But it was getting boring and I couldn't even sit on a bench because they were wet. The rain sifted down on to this grimy provincial street, uneasy with all its traffic, the lorries and cars and delivery vans nudging and shuddering from one zebra to the next; Boots the Chemist, Woolworth's, the Odeon; the white-faced shop girls and determined old women heaving their trolleys over the kerbs. Then even Ruth walked past me without a flicker of recognition and she was with Nigel Matthews again, but they weren't arm in arm because there were so many people from the houseparty in the streets today, including Holy R. probably. I turned and hobbled after them with the rolling walk I'd adopted, something like my brother's only hunched too and with a stick. Crossing at a light a nun smiled at me coming the other way and only at the last second I realized that this was Tricia Morgan who everybody said had a crush on me and I'd been avoiding her like the plague all week because she was a bit on the tubby side and the boys used to say when she put her bra on in the morning it was all a question of guesswork and she just filled up the cups with whatever was available. 'I'm going to the Woolworth's snack bar,' she hissed after me, but I didn't turn. The spies weren't supposed to fraternize with each other or it would be a dead give-away, wouldn't it – a tramp with a nun at the Woolworth's snack bar!

I followed Nigel and Ruth. I followed them up a side-street and another and another, and now they were out of the main drag she found one of those tiny telescoping women's umbrellas in her handbag, red and yellow, and they put it up and then had to walk very close together under it. Ruth had her red high-heels on and black tights and her shoes scraped and clipped along the kerb like so many sharp striking matches.

They went into a churchyard and there was a bench there with a shelter like a bus-shelter and they sat down. I hobbled round the graveyard wall to where I could watch them – excited with the bitterness I felt – and they kissed of course. She wiped the lipstick off her lips with a little finger wrapped tight in a tissue and they kissed and he held her. I thought, this is what it's like to be grown up and be betrayed, and I was terribly excited. I thought, she never really cared what Rolandson had said, it had just been an excuse and I was stupid. Then they went into the church.

So I followed them in there too, banging the door, just so as she would be able to see how damn upset I was, how guilty she was. I thought I would go in there and burst into tears in front of both of them and make a big scene. I was really boiling with anger all of a sudden and shame and all the dreams I'd had of what it might be like to put a hand inside her clothes – after we were married of course, after we were married. I went in there and they were both knelt together in a pew. I banged the door violently, tensing my-self ready, and they turned – but then Nigel suddenly burst out laughing.

'Are your teeth your own?' he said. And so I had to give them my part of the secret message, which was, 'Outer Mongolia.'

'You're supposed to stay in the street,' he laughed, 'not to hide away here. It's not fair on the others.'

Ruth said, 'Oh Richard, you do look so funny, your moustache is slipping!'

So I ran back to Woolworth's snack bar, but Tricia wasn't there.

It was my father who preached that night, before he went back to London, and I was always positively tortured with embarrassment when my father preached and all the young people could watch the nervous way he clutched his hand in his hair and they could catalogue his clichés and see his cheeks and forehead go from veiny pale, to pink, to salmon-pink and his thick old spectacles reflecting the beam of every stray light bulb. So I said I was ill: I went off up to my dormitory and lay on my bed for hours and from here I could just faintly hear them singing below and later, just very faintly, I could smell the smell of cocoa.

Adrian came up and asked me if he could borrow a couple of quid for the pub.

I gave it to him.

'Anna's trying to convert your Anne-Marie,' I said. 'I saw them talking together in town.'

'Let her.'

'It's their way of getting at you though, to convert Anne-Marie.'

'As long as she doesn't turn celibate, she can belong to any damn religion she likes.' He grinned. 'Give 'em satisfaction and you've got them where you want 'em. Doesn't matter how lame you are, it's the middle leg that counts.' He laughed his laugh and pushed out the small gingery beard he had.

'Cheer up, baldie,' he said and stumbled out. Really, it made me want to be like him the way he was always cheerful and strong. So suddenly I got up and went downstairs and found Tricia, who was in a little prayer meeting with some other girls in the chess-playing part of the tuckshop. I whispered to her and she got up and got her coat at once.

We squelched down to the pine woods and as soon as we were in a half-dry spot under the dripping trees, we kissed violently. I tried to copy the kiss Nigel Matthews had given Ruth, and Tricia put her tongue right inside my mouth which nobody had done to me before. I pushed her over on the damp ground like they do in films, but it was very clammy and uncomfortable. Then after half an hour or so she wanted us to go back and pray together that God would bless us because apparently my father had been preaching that evening that any relationship between a man and woman was okay so long as it was consecrated by God and permanent; but I said I was too tired and we could do that in the morning.

★   ★   ★

The following morning, as soon as my father had gone, Rolandson got on to my mother and he said he had definite proof now that Adrian was using a little woodshed round the back of the school to do lewd things with Anne-Marie and they really must put their foot down and stop it because he was corrupting others and taking them there too; Andy and Denise to mention only two, he said. But he didn't tell my mother it was Maggie who had told him all that – and two whole days ago.

My mother collared me after the morning meeting.

'Is it true that Adrian's taking people to that little wood-shed?'

I said I didn't know. I felt suddenly really terribly guilty, as if somehow she might have seen me with Tricia.

'I haven't been there,' I said. 'I haven't. I don't know.'

'Do you think I should be harder on him?' she demanded. Her old brown eyes fluttered in a net of wrinkles. She was lost without Father. But she didn't want to ring him and discuss it because in that case she would have to tell him what Rolandson had told her. And then there would be no peace.

I didn't know, I said. Anything.

'We've given him too much liberty, perhaps?'

I said I didn't know. Really, I didn't. She looked into my eyes very hard and sad, almost in tears, until I was sure she must see the guilt in me.

'The Lord warned us,' she said. 'That's why it was me He gave the prophecy to. We should have been harder on him, we've been nursing Satan right in our midst' – and then she saw Anne-Marie coming out of the tuckshop and went to grab hold of her.

My mother took Anne-Marie to the counselling room and talked to her for two solid hours so that she missed Rolandson's Sunday morning sermon which was on that story where Jesus casts out a vast number of devils from a man called Legion and sends them into a herd of swine so that the pigs all gallop off the end of a cliff and are dashed to pieces in the rocks and sea. In a way we all had a herd of swine inside us, he said, and it took the Lord to send them galloping away over a cliff to eternal perdition. He himself had been full of sin once, and of greed and lewd desire, and it was the Lord had torn it out of him. But the important part of the story, he said, was that after the devils had gone, the Lord had to fill the man with something to prevent more devils coming back – otherwise his soul would be like a house swept clean, but empty and vulnerable to the first passer-by. 'You cannot be neutral,' Rolandson said. 'You cannot be swept clean of sin and remain that way, still the same person. That is the insufferable arrogance of atheism and agnosticism, of the ego that pretends it can live without a spiritual master. No, once swept clean, you have to accept the Holy Spirit as master. You have to serve somebody. You must. And so the very core of your character has to change, to be transformed; the old burnt out and the new firmly planted. You must become a new person.'

Then Rolandson announced what none of us knew up to then: that Joy Kandinsky would be coming up to speak to us that evening; a woman blessed, he said, with all the charismatic gifts, and most of all perhaps with the courage to use them; and he hoped and prayed that before this day was over every one of our young hearts would be swept clean and what's more filled to bursting point with the fire of the Holy Spirit.

I went for a walk with Tricia afterwards in a thin breezy rain, under two umbrellas but as soon as we were out of sight of the house she put down hers and came under mine. She said, wasn't it good Joy Kandinsky was coming up this evening?

It was, and it wasn't, I said. I didn't really care. But then finally, like sunshine between clouds almost, a vision, it came to the front of my mind, clear as crystal, what had been forming there for month after month upon month.

'The point is I don't really want to change,' I said. 'I don't like the idea of changing.' It was so obvious.

'What?'

'I mean, I'm the way I am,' I said. 'I don't want all this changing, being transformed and reshaped and so on.'

We sauntered down this rainy road to the village and she had her arm round me under my coat.

'And Adrian's the way he is,' I said. My mind was singing with confidence – the first time for ages.

She didn't say anything.

'I mean, I like Adrian. He's a bit mean but that's the way he is. If he wasn't he wouldn't be Adrian, would he? He'd be like Anna and I wouldn't like him to be like Anna, or she like him. Anna's Anna in the end, and Adrian's Adrian. I like both of them the way they are.'

'You're too clever for me,' she said happily.

And she said softly, 'Ricky, I still think we ought to pray about what we did last night. Because I won't feel safe if it's not consecrated or holy.'

Then her bringing that up confused me all over again, because only yesterday morning I'd been despising her and everything and making the same joke the others did about her bra. And today there I was walking along with my arm inside her coat and sweater.

'I don't feel like praying about it,' I said. We turned a corner into the village and the place was grey with rain.

'I don't feel like praying at all about anything at the moment.'

She laughed, rather nervously.

'Let's go for a drink,' I said. 'They'll never ask our age.'

But when we got there they did, and we had to drink Coca-Cola.

Meanwhile my mother was still talking to Anne-Marie and my mother was so talented at talking to people and opening up their hearts that Anne-Marie was telling her now that a girl absolutely had to go to bed with her boyfriend these days because these were the sixties, not the forties, and if she didn't he would go off with somebody else who would; and anyway, she said, she couldn't really see what was wrong with it if they were in love and they used contraceptives, and she was certainly in love with Adrian. She loved him and she wanted to help him and he was only so cynical, she said, because of how bad he felt about having a club foot. People didn't realize that.

Behind her thick tresses, Anne-Marie was both timid and bold and my mother found she liked her. She liked her a lot and she was even faintly attracted to the situation the way Anne-Marie presented it; because whereas most of her girls came to her with a 'problem', Anne-Marie didn't think of it like that at all, but as a positive, romantic thing, and my mother was always attracted to romance and to the positive side of any situation. But then at the same time of course she had to think of that ugly piece of tin foil on the fresh green lawn in the early morning, and she had to remember what Father had said over the dinner table ten thousand times, that sex outside marriage, was a manifestation of Satan's power in the contemporary scene today; and then there were the words of that prophecy from her own lips, that Satan was in their midst and she hadn't used the gifts the Lord had given her.

'Try and bring him to the meeting tonight,' she said. 'I'd feel so much better if you were both Christians and got married.'

But Adrian didn't want to get married, Anne-Marie laughed. Because he would never accept anything that limited one's potential for experience in this world. To experience everything was maybe even our duty in the end, she suggested. But now she was repeating what Mother had heard already from Adrian's mouth at dinner time. She frowned.

And Anne-Marie added, 'I'm not really against marriage myself though. I mean, I wouldn't be.'

My mother asked Anne-Marie to pray with her and she did, though she didn't say anything out loud, and she said she would come to the meeting tonight and she would try to get

Adrian to come too perhaps, because she had nothing against meetings either, and it would be another experience in the end, wouldn't it?

Mother said she didn't know about that, she was sure. She went directly off to her room and stayed shut in there wrestling with the Lord over Adrian's soul for hours and hours, so that we didn't see her again until Joy Kandinsky opened the evening meeting with 'a hand-clap for Jesus'.

*   *   *

We all clapped our hands fiercely for nearly five minutes which was to show our love and appreciation and worship for the Lord, and then we sang as many as ten Fountain Trust hymns in succession with Joy Kandinsky beating a tambourine against a tubby hip and Rolandson beaming beside her.

She was dynamite, Joy Kandinsky. She wore a loose pink trouser-suit over a golden blouse and her hair was coiled above her broad face in almost a Christmas-pudding shape of black tresses – which made her look a bit ridiculous at first, and innocuous. But she was dynamite. After a moment her husky deep American voice began to cast a spell, a strange spell of attentiveness. She didn't follow a formal meeting format, with singing then sermon then open prayer then singing then finish. She mixed them up all at once together. She would start with preaching; not the blunderbuss of Rolandson, nor the old-fashioned scriptural line my father took, but a honeyed husky voice, talking about the experience of one of her friends, perhaps, being brought to the Lord, how he overcame marital problems or sexual problems or drug addiction and how the Lord banished Satan right out of his heart. And as she spoke she punctuated everything she said with ay-mens and hallelujahs and suddenly, right in the middle, she would burst out into song in a raucous, unashamedly tone-deaf voice and everybody was supposed to join in with her while Anna picked up the tune on the piano. And they did join in: they raised their arms and stamped their feet – even Alan Ingrams who was so deeply depressed about his job and Terry in his leather jacket and studs – and Joy Kandinsky said 'Ay-men!' and 'Hallelujah!', and then continued with her story, or plunged into prayer perhaps. While us in the Youth Fellowship, we exchanged ecstatic smiles, of acceptance, of forgiveness, of friendship, and there was an emotional power so strong in that room and so persuasive, you felt it like a physical pressure, like being underwater, or caught in a rising wind. I sat next to Tricia and held her hand tight.

We sang that hymn, 'The Lord of the Dance', and Joy Kandinsky said, 'Anybody that can really dance, why don't you come right out here and dance before the Lord!' – and one of the girls who studied dance at the same college Adrian went to, she went out to the front and did one of those funny contemporary dances that are half ballet and half pop. We clapped and sang and she danced on the shabby school stage in front of cupboards full of sports trophies, twisting and turning in the space between Rolandson and Joy Kandinsky; quite a sexy dance it was because she had tight jeans on and a loose blouse that her breasts jumped up and down in. She finished doing a bend backwards over a chair, her legs wide apart and her arms thrown out, as if prostrate beneath the power of someone above, beneath God, bent back and back and back, till it seemed she must break or fall. And then the hymn was finished.

Joy Kandinsky started on about her friends again. What made her so good at this was that the stories were really interesting and modern. There was one about somebody who refused to come to Jesus because he wouldn't accept the notion of chastity or marriage with one woman, and he was young and handsome and could have as many pretty women as he chose. 'He took and picked as it suited him,' she said, looking round at the young men in the room. 'Brethren, I tell you, that man was so popular and handsome you could hardly believe it. My word, he took and picked as he chose and he was notorious!' But then it seems this character finally fell deeply in love with someone. He fell deeply, deeply in love so that there was only one woman he wanted in the whole wide world and all the rest now were as dust and ashes for him, nothing more.

'And you know what the problem was?' she said in a softer voice. 'You know what the little old problem was this time?' The American woman smiled her tubby smile and folded her arms firmly over big breasts in the golden blouse. 'The problem was that this woman was married, yes, and even if she was attracted to our friend, even if for just a moment she felt maybe a throb of love or passion for that man, yet she was a strong and Christian woman and she had no intention of betraying a lifetime's trust for the awful pleasure of a moment.'

'Ay-men!' Rolandson said.

'And it is these moments that make us doubt God, is it not, brothers and sisters! Isn't it just these moments, when His Law falls like an axe into the heart of our deepest and strongest, and, we think perhaps our best desires? It is not in the midst of common sin that we doubt the Lord. No, in the squalor and evil of our little sins we see Him more clearly than ever, as an example, a hope of freedom, a conscience, hallelujah! But when the Word of God comes down and crushes what we in our arrogance and ignorance have set up

97

as good and desirable – our career perhaps, our love for a married woman, or man – it is then that we deny God and we hate even the thought of Him, even the sound of His blessed Name.'

Silence. She walked a while up and down on the stage with a little white hand over her mouth. 'I wonder,' she said, half smiling, softly, 'I wonder if there isn't someone here tonight in the same position, someone whom the Lord wants so much to liberate?'

A tiny thrill sharpened the edge of the emotions already teeming in that musty room. And then she started again.

This friend of hers, it seemed, unable to seduce the married woman, fell into despair and he tried to go back to his old libertine's life, but it meant nothing to him now. It was as dust and ashes in his mouth. And he used to spend all his days thinking of this woman and watching her and following her. He thought of nothing else. So then he decided he would kill her husband. He bought a gun and he waited for the right moment. He waited at the bottom of her drive for the moment when her husband would drive off to work.

Joy Kandinsky paused and held her nose for a moment between finger and thumb, her face grim. 'Despair!' she said. 'Brethren, I'm telling you, when we fall into the sin of despair, when we fall beyond even the normal selfish reckonings and calculations of mankind, there is no telling to what lengths we may go, what crimes we may commit. Our friend bought a gun. He went to kill. He was not the first, nor, I'm afraid, brethren, will he be the last. He waited there on a bright California day at the end of her drive. Waited and waited. And the car came down the track and our friend raised his gun, his finger trembling on the trigger. But at that final moment, brethren, thanks be to Almighty God, at that final moment he couldn't do it. He simply couldn't pull that trigger. And so he set off home to shoot himself. Because the world held nothing for this man any more. His evil courage had failed him and he set off home to kill himself.' She smiled the sad smile again, and there wasn't a person in the room now who wasn't on the edge of his seat to know what happened to this libidinous American.

She sighed. 'But the condemned man tends to drag out his trip to the execution place. Yes, children, even the most despairing of us, praise the Lord, cannot help but see the goodness in God's light and life. And so it was, turning aside from the road here and there, to a café, a burger-house, a cinema, spinning it out through the early evening, putting it off and off, that this man finally turned into a meeting of mine, and the Lord pointed him out to me. 'Speak to him,' the Lord said, 'Speak to that sinner.' And after the meeting, brethren, I went and spoke to him and with the help of Almighty God I was able to show that man how Satan had tricked him and trapped him and drawn him to the very brink of that dark precipice down which so many have fallen.' She paused. 'And you know how Satan had tricked him, brothers and sisters? Do you know how? I wonder if you do?' Her voice fell to a husky hush. 'I wonder if you know. He tricked him the way he tricks so many of us. He had led our friend to believe that sex and romance was everything in life. He had blinkered his eyes so that he saw nothing beyond his lusts and his desires. No, he barely saw the world at all beyond those lusts. Certainly he had no inkling of the ways of God and the path He in His love and mercy prepares for us. And when I showed that man how blinkered he was, when I showed him how narrow was his vision of life and satisfaction, it was as if he had been set free from a prison, yea, *liberated, hallelujah!*, from the prison of his own lusts and desires.'

She paused a long moment now and amongst the whispered ay-mens and hallelujahs, she lifted her white stubby hands and pressed them against her temples and the sticky coiffeur that towered above, and she closed her eyes.

'I feel the Lord is moving me toward this discourse tonight,' she said. 'I feel His power leading me.'

'Ay-men!' Rolandson said, and then my mother, who was sitting at the back of the stage, started singing, 'And Should It Be', so that everyone joined in, but strangely softly today and only for a single verse, because of a kind of electric stillness there was behind our voices. And after the singing there was stillness, and I gripped Tricia's wrist.

'The Lord is moving me toward this discourse.' She didn't open her eyes but raised her arms in supplication. 'May Thy will prevail, oh Lord!'

'Ah-men,' my mother said. 'Praise be to God,' and she had her face buried in her hands. I looked for Anne-Marie and found the back of her head next to Maggie's in the front row. To our right the great dark panes of glass held all our our tense profiles against a glossy black behind, where Adrian would be, enjoying himself somewhere, I thought. Because he wouldn't let the fact that Anne-Marie was here bother him overmuch, and he certainly wouldn't come himself. And I thought how different Adrian was from the man in Joy Kandinsky's story; how Adrian wasn't beaten and never would be, because everything always went well for Adrian. The woman in the story would have left her husband for Adrian.

Joy Kandinsky opened her eyes.

'Sex is our weak spot, brothers and sisters. Dressed in all the armour of God, sex is still a weak spot. There will be many of you here tonight who have discovered that already, to your fear and peril; many of you here tonight who find yourself fascinated by the body of another and who live dwarfed and terrified by that fascination, like one drawn to the awful edge of the cliff, dizzy with vertigo ready to throw himself off' – a pause – 'But let us not be afraid, children. Sex is our weak spot, but oh let us not be afraid. Ay-men. Our God is not a God of fear.' She pursed her lips, changed her voice. 'So then, are we to cut sex out altogether, as some would teach? No, that is not God's way. Sex is God's gift. Let us by all means be lovers! Hallelujah! Let us be lovers as long as we can. Ay-men! But at the same time let us keep sex in its place, a secondary thing, a part of marriage always, of ourselves consecrated to the Lord. This is what the story here tells us. Put God first and foremost and all the rest must fall into place and will be holy.'

A pause again and muttered ay-mens. She stood tubby and tall in the pink trouser-suit, her face beaming now. A great sigh passed over the gathering; but still there was that electric stillness in the air that seemed somehow concentrated, intensified in the gloss of black reflections to our right, those great dark windows, as if Satan himself might be invested there and our Satanic self – and beyond that, Adrian. A moth fluttered into the lightshade, irritating tiny uncertain shadows about the walls.

'Sex is the weak spot. It is so clear – and slowly, brethren, but very slowly, the Lord is moving us in this discourse. Yes, there are those of you here this evening, I see you all so plainly, there are those of you quite blinded with lust, those of you who live in lust and the delight of touching – a girl's soft breasts, the curve of a young man's belly – there are those of you who even here in this place and time set apart for prayer and meditation – those of you who have sinned against yourselves and God and abused your bodies in the pit of fornication.'

She stretched out her arms from the pink jacket into the ringing stillness of the room.

'It is not the worst of sins, brethren, fornication. It is not irremediable. And the Lord is kind. Hallelujah! There is no cause to despair. So those of you – and you know who you are – oh you know – why don't you come out here now and confess yourselves to God and put all that behind you – the prison of lust and blind desire and the pleasure that aches and cries out in its sinfulness. Walk out here now! Wash yourselves in His blood. Come!'

And they went. There was a dead silence first, like the silence at those Friday prayer meetings, the silence of each one waiting for another. And then there was a rustling and scraping of chairs and one by one they went. Ruth went first, leading Nigel Matthews, hand in limp hand and heads downcast. The rest of the gathering, heads bowed in prayer, lifted their eyes, straining to see who it was, sighing with surprise. And then another scraping of chairs. I held Tricia's wrist and I dug in my fingernails so it must have hurt and hurt. 'Don't!' I said.

And Andy and Denise went, and then even Anne-Marie, covering her face with her hair; Anne-Marie went forward and my mother said, 'Praise the Lord. Praise, oh praise the Lord!'

And finally Alan Ingrams went, who had never been known even to speak to a girl, let alone touch one, because he was always so depressed about his job and his acne. He went and knelt with the others at the front.

We sang 'Raised on a Dove's Wings', with a kind of suppressed and tortured ecstasy. Anne-Marie raised her hand. She was saved.

'There are still those of you who have not come. Come now and be blessed while there is still time – "For verily I say unto you, the hour is coming and is even at hand when the Lord will sit in judgment upon us all." ' She paused on a deathly silence. 'And, brethren, we read, "In that day the one shall be taken and the other shall be left." Yea, the Scripture tells us, "There will be two people working together in the fields" – two people lying together in the marriage bed perhaps – "and the one shall be taken and the other shall be left." The Lord will be kind, yes He will, but just He must also be. And the wages of sin is *death!*'

Then Tricia shook my arm free in a single fierce wild gesture and ran to the front streaming with tears. And it was me that was left. I was even amazed my feet didn't move of their own accord and take me to the front with her. But another voice inside me said, 'I'm damned if I'm going up there. Damned! I'm damned,' and behind even that voice those three awful words started croaking away as ever, 'Ravishnah, homorrah homorrah – ravishnah, homorrah homorrah!' and they seemed to hold me back rather than push me forward, so that I didn't know if they were sacred or profane and I felt sick.

Arms outstretched, Joy Kandinsky lay white hands on them all at the front. Her voice was honey and cocoa.

'The Lord tells me there are still two or three more of you. But Satan is strong.'

The room waited in that steadily intensifying silence that was like something stretching out tighter and tighter between us. And the moth banged against the light bulb trembling the shadows on the wall.

My mother prayed out loud in tongues, and Rolandson too, nodding and shaking his head for a moment quite furiously.

Anna said very loud, 'Give not the victory unto Satan, oh Lord, but tonight let Thy Will triumph!' and everybody shouted, 'Ay-men!'

Yet the silence, returning, was not lessened nor weakened by these outbreaks. It was intensified rather, it was stretched out tight as a drum-skin now for the preacher to beat upon when she would. And I was clutching my rickety chair like a man in a gale clawing a cliff-face.

Her voice was very soft. 'There are one or two more of you. The Lord is leading me in this discourse. And there is one of you particularly here tonight who is suffering and screaming inside for sins far greater than these we have seen so far. Sex is the weak point. But the Lord is kind. He is generous and kind. Nothing is unforgivable.'

She stopped, and then in a perfectly natural voice, she said, 'But let me tell you another story.' And the tension rushed from the room like wind from a burst balloon.

*   *   *

We settled back on our chairs and she told another story, and now in the relative calm you realized how rain had begun to beat and lash on those shiny panes harder than ever, splintering all our reflections there in trails and smears of dark light.

She knew a man, she said, who had wanted to be a woman. This was back in San Francisco. His name was Elmer. Elmer was a young black at the university and he wanted to be a woman.

She rubbed her hands together, thinking, looking for the right word to continue, and we were still as church mice listening, suburban middle class the most of us, in this Surrey boarding school, listening to this story of the young black in San Francisco who wanted to be a woman. Those who had been out to the front were back in their seats now with heads buried in their hands and somebody was weeping quietly.

'The Lord is beckoning somebody tonight,' she said quietly. 'The Lord is looking for a great victory tonight. But Satan is strong.' She watched us as she spoke, eyes moving gently from person to person, the smile soft and sad in a piggy face.

'Elmer couldn't face his male position in society. He felt misplaced. He felt unequal to the man's role as breadwinner, lover, and father. He felt no attraction for the bodies of women, nor any healthy delight in their company. He struggled with these feelings, brethren, I want to tell you, I *knew* Elmer and I knew he struggled, he fought with himself – but the feelings were strong inside him. He simply felt no attraction to women. It was men instead that attracted him: the broadness of a man's shoulders, the slimness of his hips, the firmness of a man's flesh around the buttocks and belly, these were the visions that filled his dreams.'

Stinging silence again when she stopped – and the tension had started again. Every eye avoided every other.

'Perhaps I use words you don't expect, or words you don't want to hear at a religious meeting. But children, we must never deny the fearful strength of these feelings that invade us, of the lusts that invade and seize us. Let us not pretend that the devil is weak or the world brighter and better and more innocent than it is. This old world runs and throngs with dark currents, lit only by the single light of our Saviour, the Lord Jesus Christ.'

A muttering of ay-mens.

'Elmer loved the bodies of men. And yet strangely he felt his own body was disgusting. He felt he was a stranger in his own body, an alien, and he starved it and abused it and showed it no respect, because he didn't want to be a man himself. He wanted to *have* men.' She stopped. 'Children, let us bow our heads a moment. I feel the Lord is moving me, there is one of you here tonight who suffers in the same way Elmer suffered. There is one of you here, man or woman, I don't know, who feels like a stranger in his body and is kicking and screaming to be out.'

We were jolted by this sudden new tension, this twist; we were breathless almost with the pressing dark of those windows and the moth fluttering in tassels of the light shade. The room was suffocating.

She smiled. 'Elmer struggled a little while and then he gave way to these feelings. He accepted his lust for male bodies and became a homosexual, revelling in perverted pleasure. But he found no satisfaction, brethren; as none of us will ever find satisfaction outside of the way God has laid down for us.'

'Ay-men,' Rolandson said, and even he had his head in his hands now.

'Don't be afraid, whoever you are who are suffering. The Lord gave His Son for you in blood and agony on the cross that you might be set *free*. Hallelujah!'

'*Ay-men!*'

A shiver passed across the room and we felt all, every one of us, accused, guilty, and just waiting for somebody to release us with a confession that would do for all.

'Elmer sank to the lowest of the low, he indulged in every unnameable act; and *still* he couldn't shake off the disgust he felt for his own body, and the strangeness of it. He began to want to be a woman. He went to the campus doctor and tried to explain, but the man wouldn't listen. He told him to go away and pull himself together.'

She paused, her arms folded in the pink jacket again over the golden blouse and great maternal breasts. Her face was quite piggy, but kind too in an American way.

'Brethren, let us never be guilty of turning a deaf ear when a sufferer is trying to confess. Let us never be embarrassed to hear the sins of another. We need only turn our eyes to the secrets of our own hearts to find as bad or worse within.'

'Ay-men, Lord Jesus!' It was Rolandson.

'So don't be afraid whoever you are here tonight, suffering. The Lord is on your side, fighting for you. We are all on your side.'

'Hallelujah!'

My mother said ay-men, for the first time, and somebody was praying softly somewhere in tongues, a sound like a rustle among leaves. Tricia had her head down on her knees beside me and when she'd come back to her seat she'd refused to catch my eye.

'Elmer tried to kill himself. He cut his throat but by chance one of the janitors at the dormitory found him in a pool of blood in his room. He survived. Then in hospital he saw a psychiatrist who wanted to help him, who arranged for him to have a sex change, to have his body mutilated and torn and pumped full of hormones to resemble, in hopeless mockery, a woman's.'

Somebody cried out, '*No*, Lord!'

She paused. 'Brethren, there are many non-Christians who are good-hearted and will reach out their arms to help. But what they in their blindness and pride simply will not understand is that man does not *have* the answer to every problem. . . .'

'No, Lord.'

'. . . that you cannot solve a problem like Elmer's problem simply by mauling his body into the shape of a woman's. For a man is not a piece of plastic to be reheated and re-moulded as we will – no, he bears in every lineament the imprint of *God!*'

'Hallelujah!'

'And so for you who are suffering here this evening, it is

only the Lord Jesus who can help you. Only our dear Lord Jesus who shed his precious warm blood for you.'

'Ay-men.'

The moth was beating in a frenzy against the bulb itself now, and the way she told her story, so slow and interrupted, it was like a kind of torture.

'Just before the operation in the City Hospital of Los Angeles, Elmer tried to kill himself again. He took a bottleful of amphetamines. Because he *knew* inside himself that a mere operation at the hands of a clever man was a mockery of his problem. But praise the Lord he failed again and this time in the hospital he came to the attention of a certain black pastor who recognized at once the work of the Devil. And he asked me to go and see Elmer.'

The soft voice praying in tongues had risen slightly to an audible gabble. I was stripping little pieces of skin away from my thumbnail till it bled.

'I haven't time, children,' Joy Kandinsky said – her voice had changed again – 'to tell you all I discovered in quiet prayer with Elmer at his bedside: to tell you how his father died very early and his young mother brought him up alone, and how, desperate with loneliness, she flirted with her son and how she invited him as a young man even into her bed – God forgive her! No, I can only tell you that Satan will use any weak spot, any chink in our armour to launch his venom into us. And for Elmer and his mother, as for so many of us, sex was that weak spot. Sex and loneliness. And once he has found his chink, the Lord of Darkness, he will not cease until he has destroyed us, until he has rotted every fibre of our being and brought us to the very *Gates of Hell*!'

'God be with us!' Nigel Matthew cried. The gabbling of tongues again. Somebody dropped a chorus book but it barely even dented the tension.

'And what did I tell Elmer? What message is there, brethren, what message for a sufferer of this kind?' She sighed, arms raised, eyes watering with tears. 'I told him his body was the *House of God*! I told him it was a holy mansion and the abode of angels, and it was Satan, *Satan*, brethren, who had turned him against that house and all it stood for; Satan who was so eager to raze that precious palace to the ground – just as he is so eager to do the same to somebody here this evening.'

'Get thee behind me, Satan!' Rolandson said. Another voice was added to the tongues so that the murmur swelled and pressed and Joy Kandinsky had to raise her voice, louder and louder.

'I told him he must learn to *love* what the Lord had made and accept it as his home, his *home*, brothers and sisters . . .'

'Hallelujah!'

'And, man or woman, whoever you are here tonight suffering from this same and terrible disease, I tell you the same, your body is the very House of God! Nay, it is a palace, the palace of the Most High. And I ask you here in the presence of His church militant upon earth to confess the horror of your life, and, like Elmer before you, to learn to accept yourself and to accept the role God has prepared for you in society, and to live in happiness and peace and joy! Yes, even in joy!'

'Praise the Lord!' Anna said.

'Oh yes, yes – ay-men!'

'Come out and confess yourself! Perhaps you are afraid. Of course you are afraid. All of us are afraid sometimes. But God loves you. He will be kind.'

'Praise be to God for this His Word.'

Someone began to sing, 'Surely goodness and mercy . . .', and we all sang it in soft urgent voices, '. . . And I shall dwell in the House of the Lord forever, and I shall feast at the table set for me-e-e.'

Joy Kandinsky cut into our singing in a perfectly calm, perfectly sane voice. 'Come forth, oh lost one, and confess yourself.'

Then silence. But total silence. Even the moth seemed to have beaten out its life against the bulb and was fallen dead upon the floor somewhere. The bright black windows watched. And I wondered a moment whether it was me. Whether I was homosexual. Did I make such an effort to spy upon women just to cover it up from myself? Should I go forward? What would happen if no one went forward? And I wanted whoever it was to confess themselves at once, at once, to have it over with. But then how did she *know* there was someone here who felt like that? How? Had God actually told her in her mind? Or was she just going on the law of averages? One in every group. Or was that the Devil speaking in me? 'Ravishnah, homorrah homorrah!' I couldn't get rid of that voice. It came back and back.

Silence.

'The devil is strong,' she whispered. 'Perhaps this will not be the night.'

'No!' Rolandson shouted. 'Get thee behind me, Satan!'

'Let the Lord triumph tonight,' Anna said.

My mother shouted, 'Ay-men, Thine be the victory, oh Lord!'

Tricia beside me was very agitated and shaking and quite suddenly she dropped forward off her chair on to her knees and began to pray very loud in tongues, a running gurgling babble of soft, sometimes even pleasant sounds. Her shoulders shook. And I wondered, could it be her? Could it be her, who had wanted to be with me only to hide the fact that really she loved women? Or was everybody thinking it was themselves or their partners? Or was it even Rolandson who was still unmarried at thirty-four? That might explain everything.

Then suddenly everybody was kneeling and praying aloud in tongues for whoever the poor soul was, a cacophonous clashing sound of voices, each running round and round a few strange garbled syllables, words without any detectable meaning, unless to God and Satan. I tried to pray too. I said, 'Lord Jesus, please help whoever the poor soul is if there really is one.' But it was useless, and all I wanted really was to be out of there, to have it finished. I felt slowly, but slowly, a great loathing rise within me and I looked towards the dark panes where Adrian would be, stomping through the rain or leaning up against a bar.

Joy Kandinsky was praying in tongues too now. Very loud. Her booming American voice clamoured and droned – her two short arms raised and shaking to the dusty ceiling, fingers outstretched. She stopped and abruptly everybody stopped.

'I command thee, Satan,' she shouted. She yelled it at the top of her voice. 'I command thee, Satan, in the name of the Most High Almighty God, who after his death upon the cross did battle with thee and smashed the very gates of Hell, I *command* thee now to come forth from that poor victim you have claimed – come forth I tell you!'

A moment's aching silence. Tingling and ringing with challenge. But nothing. No one moved. And so the tongues began again, rising and rising like a threatening gale, Alan Ingrams's head waggling furiously from side to side in agitation. I wondered whether it was Alan Ingrams perhaps? He seemed a bit queer the way he could hang around you sometimes.

Until, in the midst of that rising clamour then, a figure in the front row hurled itself forward, prostrate and writhing on the floor. And it was Maggie.

She shouted inarticulately, writhing there as if in terrific pain: and Joy Kandinsky and my mother, Rolandson and Anna, all rushed to grab her and raise her to her feet.

Everybody burst into song. We sang 'Raised on a Dove's Wings', and some people were almost wild with ecstasy, with release, and they turned to embrace their neighbours and hugged and hugged. But Tricia stayed knelt on the bare floorboards, praying and trembling.

Joy Kandinsky started singing 'To God be the Glory, great things He hath done . . .', so we all sang that too and now some people stomped their feet on the floor. The preacher's face was a great piggy pink beam, her singing almost a shout, 'So loved He the world that He gave us His Son.'

Held between the four of them, Maggie howled and shook. Rain lashed the windows. And then as soon as the singing stopped she began to talk very loud.

'I wanted to be a man, dear God forgive me. I wanted sex with a woman. Every woman tempts me. Anna tempts me. Anne-Marie. Every woman.'

She spoke in that strong Cockney accent.

Joy Kandinsky put her arm around her as she spoke, praying and muttering – 'Don't be afraid. We all love you. Liberate yourself, confess yourself.'

'I thought Mrs Bowen had saved me,' Maggie went on, her voice almost sobbing but strangely controlled too, and her round face was strangely bright with that quick Cockney brightness she always had. 'I thought she had saved me and then I realized she hadn't and I was in love with Anna. And I resisted. Until finally the Devil came to me in the shape of Adrian and he said it wasn't wrong my lust, and every experience should be tried at least once. And so I made love with many women and also men to see if I could change. And I made love with Adrian and Anne-Marie both together.'

Anne-Marie shouted, 'No, no! It's not true!'

'Be silent, Satan!' Joy Kandinsky said. 'The Lord is with her in her confession.'

'But it's not true!' Anne-Marie was weeping. 'We never did that.'

Rolandson went over and took hold of the small girl's shoulders in his hands because she was shaking violently. His great blond eyebrows bristled.

'Don't be afraid to confess yourself,' he said. 'We all have sinned.'

Maggie said 'We had sex together all three of us for the experience.'

'God forgive them,' my mother wailed in tears.

The murmur of tongues had begun again.

'Is this true?' Joy Kandinsky demanded of Anne-Marie. She smiled but was threatening somehow in her pink trouser-suit. 'Tell us it is true. For the Lord will not hold it lightly if one should speak falsely and bear false witness before His congregation.'

Rolandson gripped the weeping girl, small, with beautiful chestnut hair pulled down around her face: the girl with the small pointed breasts, who made those sounds with Adrian in his room, who had held him with Maggie beneath my window. Her voice was barely audible.

'No, I mean, I don't know. I don't think so. But we were all drunk together sometimes. I . . .' She tailed off to the murmuring of other tongues and that rain lashed against the window.

'The Devil tempted me in the shape of Adrian,' Maggie howled. Anna hugged her. 'He tempted me and I fell.'

'May God in His mercy forgive you all,' Joy Kandinsky

said – and I knew then that when Adrian came back they were going to get him. They were going to get him, because they couldn't not get him after all that had been said. It might have been said on purpose – and I should warn him.

★   ★   ★

With Anne-Marie's mumblings accepted as a confession the meeting now ended quite abruptly: so abruptly it took us by surprise. We were dazed. Because it seemed that for all her fervour Joy Kandinsky had kept the corner of a professional eye on her watch and now she was already a bit late for the last train back to London. So we sang all eight verses of 'And Should It Be', right through twice and then she hurried off with Nigel Matthews who would drive her to the station, and all the rest of us stayed and sang some more hymns before the meeting ended and Rolandson said a prayer thanking God for Joy Kandinsky and petitioning him that she wouldn't miss her train. Then most people went off for cocoa and biscuits and Merv and Madge records in the tuckshop; but Maggie and Anne-Marie, with my mother, Rolandson and Anna, all trooped off to the counselling room to be Baptized or Rebaptized in the Spirit.

I prowled. Where was Adrian? And what time would he come back? They were going to get him. I went back to the assembly hall, dark and empty, and pressed my nose against the cold panes. He was out there. Doing what? Having fun of course, which was what he always did in his odd cynical way. I tried to think of Adrian, his proud face and straight nose – his clear clear eyes, and the club foot that made him roll when he walked and that meant he could never really run or jump or play the sports that other people played with teams and running. I tried to think of the odd twist of that

114

ankle, the shrivelled look of the whole thing and the deadness of the toes – of the way he never wanted you to see it when he undressed. Where was he now? He was in the pub of course, leaning over the bar, trying to chat up a barmaid with his slow, dry voice, cracking dry jokes. And I thought I loved him in a way and I should warn him – but I couldn't. I felt paralysed.

I should warn him. But perhaps that was Satan speaking? I was paralysed, my cheek pressed on the window and my own dark reflection glued there on the other side, blurred with rain. I didn't believe in God and Satan, not really, and yet I didn't have the courage to disbelieve. I put the palms of my hands against the window till the blood went out of them and they were white. How had the American woman known, *known* there was somebody in the meeting with that problem? Or was it a safe bet in any crowd of young people? And Maggie? Obviously that was the problem, her problem – everything fell into place – and yet somehow I couldn't help feeling she had staged the whole thing, timed it and done it on purpose, and it wasn't to do with God at all. She hated men, hated Adrian and wanted to get him. She hated all our family because we had helped her, or tried to. I pulled my face back and stared the rainy reflection in the eyes. I must warn him.

I opened the french window and went out on the terrace. It was soaking and fresh and tremendously breathable. I wanted to be soaked and completely fresh and a million million miles away from this place. I breathed in deep lungfuls as if it were the whole dark sky I wanted to swallow. I must warn Adrian – directly. Because there was no such person as Satan – how could there be? – only people with their heads full of this or that.

I looked out at the muddy path down to the pine woods.

He would be there, in the village, in the pub; and I started across the terrace, but then somebody called me from behind, coming after me, and it was Tricia.

'I've been looking for you everywhere,' she said. She was breathless. 'Come in out of the rain. You'll catch your death.' She giggled nervously.

I came in and there was her round white face in the dark. She took my hand but I shook her off. I felt suddenly furious.

'What's wrong? Can't we even touch each other?'

'Not if you have to go into paroxysms of confession every time,' I said.

And I said, 'God! It's ridiculous you know, stupid!' But she was silent, hanging her head a little. She was quite surprisingly beautiful then for a moment in that half-dark, her face pastel and clear and the bowed neck fine like fine marble. I hadn't thought she might be so beautiful.

'I feel like a great big bloody idiot,' I said, and I turned to go, stumbling over a chair.

'Stay,' she said. 'Oh please stay a moment.'

When I stopped she came after me and she reached up and tried to kiss me on the lips but I pushed her away.

'It's bloody stupid,' I said.

She began to cry, so I stayed again. She said why couldn't we just pray together before God so it would be concentrated – 'I mean consecrated,' she said, and giggled nervously again, still breathless, wiping her eyes. She said all she wanted was to feel it was right. She got so worked up in those meetings sometimes she didn't know where she was.

'You're not the only one,' I said.

'But I'm not a prude, Ricky, I'm not.'

I was angry and confused. 'I don't know,' I said. 'It seems stupid to me, all of it. Let's just forget it. We're only fifteen.

You don't consecrate things when you're fifteen,' and I turned another time to go.

She said very softly, 'Ricky?'

'Yes?'

'We can do it properly now if you want. I found where to get . . .' – she turned away so there was all her dark hair on her shoulders – '. . . where to get the things. We could make love right here. I only wanted that we should pray a bit first because . . .'

I ran out of the room banging and stumbling against chairs in the dark. I ran. I must warn Adrian. This was crazy! And of course he wouldn't use the path through the pine woods tonight. It was too muddy. He would come up the main road. I must go out the main door and wait for him on the road there, down the drive.

But in the corridor going past the counselling room, there was my mother coming out in tears and grim at the same time hiding her big pale face in a handkerchief.

'Richard!' she cried, and she grabbed me and hugged me. 'Richard, you must pray for your brother!' she said.

I didn't say a word. I put my arms round her and she squeezed me. She smelt of her scent and handkerchiefs full of tears. 'Pray for him, Richard!'

My throat was dry. I couldn't speak.

'Rolandson has had a word from the Lord to say he is possessed by a devil and we have been refusing to admit it just because he's our son. It's my fault,' she said. 'All my fault. His presence is disturbing the whole Fellowship. I should have seen it ages ago.'

Then finally I got out that I would pray for him, because she said they had to exorcize him tonight.

She went back into the counselling room and I walked on to the main entrance. But I didn't go out. I didn't go down to the drive and wait. Because I thought again now, after being in my mother's trembling arms like that, pressed against her breast, I thought, perhaps it was Satan prompting me to warn him. Perhaps they were right. And after all he *had* started orgies with two girls together, hadn't he? – making those noises he'd made with Anne-Marie, only worse. Which was disgusting. And Joy Kandinsky *had* known there was somebody in that group who had that problem, hadn't she? She must have been guided by God. How else could she have known? And who was I to interfere? I argued with myself and shouted inside myself, but I didn't go down the drive to the pine woods and the road.

★   ★   ★

And so it was they got him. They caught him round midnight, half-drunk at the doorway, and Rolandson and Anna and Maggie, they dragged him forcibly to the counselling room while my mother watched. I heard Adrian shouting from a distance and struggling and all the while Rolandson dragged him he said through his teeth – 'Get thee behind me, Satan! In the Name of the Lord Jesus Christ, get thee behind me!'

I went outside to watch in at the window. Partly I was just screaming inside myself to be a million miles away from my family and that houseparty and Ruth and Tricia: and yet I was compelled by the window and by the struggle within, and I had to watch for my brother's sake. There were curtains here but I found a crack and stood there squinting in from the pouring rain.

It was a smaller room, the counselling room, and I think in term-time the staff must have used it for their private dining place, because there was just one long dark polished-wood table in the middle and then cupboards about the walls, full of dinner sets behind glass doors, and a huge gloomy portrait of some nineteenth-century headmaster: he had his lips pressed together and cheeks puffed out, and he held a sherry glass, watching dourly over the scene where they tried to exorcize my brother.

They had physically to hold him down because he was a bit drunk and furious of course and struggling: and the more he carried on like this, the more they were convinced he was possessed by the Devil and Rolandson shouted, 'Get thee behind me, Satan, we bind thee in the Name of the Lord Jesus Christ and command thee to come forth.'

'Oh bugger off!' Adrian screamed. 'For Christ's sake, let me go to bed, will you, fucking lunatics. Let me go to bed, Christ!'

They had never heard him swear before. They were shocked.

'Leave me alone, Jesus!'

'Take not the Name of the Lord thy God in vain,' Anna intoned. 'For the Lord will not hold him guiltless in the Day of Judgment, who takes His Name in vain.'

'Face-ache,' Adrian said.

Mother stood at the side, weeping and muttering. 'Forgive me, Lord, forgive me, Lord. Thine be the victory tonight, Lord. Thine be the victory tonight.'

He made another big effort to be free, using his one good leg to kick Rolandson in the ankle. The big clergyman stumbled and they crashed together against a cupboard with Anna holding on. Glass smashed, sudden and brittle, and as they rolled off, a pile of plates tumbled to the floor, shooting slithering fragments across the boards.

'Fucking marvellous,' Adrian shouted, his face smothered in hair. 'Who's going to pay?' So then they struggled all the more, until finally, heaving and panting, they were able to force him down on his back on the table, each one holding an arm or a leg, pinning him quite violently. He was beaten: he rested there, gasping for breath, and their eyes about him, even my mother's, were burning bright with a sort of wildness I had never imagined before, a fierce kind of triumph in their panting. Maggie's face was quite crimson with battle.

'Thou hast *bound* him!' Rolandson cried. 'Praise the Lord!'

They held him pinned down on the teacher's dinner table, panting everybody.

'What's it to be, burnt offering or circumcision?' Adrian croaked. But he was scared. You could hear he was.

'We're trying to help you,' Anna said. 'Don't be so cynical.'

They breathed over him, Rolandson's face pumping with red and he had a great silver cross on a silver chain round his neck: Adrian lifted his head, looked around, let it fall back.

'Take a look out of the window. Aren't you supposed to find a lamb there or something at this stage, the alternative sacrifice you know, bleeding sheep.'

Nobody actually turned to the window and yet I moved away abruptly. I felt he was appealing to me in some way. I felt I was involved. And quite spontaneously, I really did say a prayer for him – it must have been the first spontaneous prayer I'd said for ages. 'Don't let them hurt him, Lord,' I prayed. 'Don't let them change him. I love him like he is. Don't let them hurt him.' And then I wondered if I could still really be a Christian if I didn't want them to change Adrian. And if I wasn't a Christian, then I wondered who really I could be praying to like this. Because it felt more like praying than ever before.

Mother said, 'Adrian, the Lord has shown us your sin here

tonight. He has moved Anne-Marie to speak before the whole congregation . . .'

'Ay-men,' Rolandson said.

'. . . about your awful fornication, which Satan tricked me briefly to think of as love and romance but which the Lord has shown us tonight is nothing more than dust and ashes. And Maggie has spoken too of the orgies between you and her and Anne-Marie and the . . .'

'What!'

My mother was having to grit her teeth to say the words, to overcome the years of silence and all the dark imaginings she'd struggled with that had never reached her tongue – the girl's dirty underwear in the wash and his door closed all Christmas. Maggie was silent, her face set fierce, but Anna had begun to speak low in tongues. I wondered where Anne-Marie was.

'The sexual orgies you had together,' Mother said, 'lesbian and heterosexual together, lascivious and foul!' The way she got it out, face full of blood and panting, stuttering, it was as if it was herself, not him, she was exorcizing of all that foulness.

'First I've heard about it,' Adrian said.

'Degrading, Satanic lust.'

'Sounds exciting. Tell me more,' he said.

Then Rolandson slapped him across the face. He didn't spare him at all, but used his great heavy hand and slapped him across the side of the face and Adrian shouted in pain. For a moment he struggled wildly, but with no hope against those four. He called Rolandson a fucking bastard.

'*Silence*, Satan!' Rolandson shouted. He stood enormously tall in his long black cassock with the silver cross swinging on its chain round his neck from the motion of the blow.

'We're trying to help you,' Anna said. 'You'll feel so much

better afterwards. Free!' And she started speaking in tongues again.

'Babbler,' Adrian said. 'Half-wit,' and he made his little demon's hiss that he had enjoyed making so much recently. 'You're all nuts.'

Rolandson hit him again.

In the rain I was burning with embarrassment and guilt and shame. I swung away from the window and stamped in the mud on the sward where three days before Maggie had found that tiny piece of tin-foil, or said she had. I stamped and stamped in the mud. 'Don't let them hurt him, Lord!' I prayed. '*Please* don't let them hurt him!'

When I went back he was bleeding slightly at the corner of his mouth.

'And the Lord has shown us you are possessed by a devil,' Mother was saying, 'who is determined to break up our Fellowship, and we must use our spiritual gifts to exorcize you. There is nothing to fear. We all love you.'

'Zap!' Adrian said. But Rolandson lifted his hand again and he was silent.

So then they all began to pray, first normally, out loud, for Adrian and his soul and so on, that Satan wouldn't harden his heart, and then they began to pray in tongues getting louder and louder, until finally Rolandson broke out, 'We *command* thee, Beelzebub, in the Name of the Lord Jesus Christ, to leave this young man,' and he held up the cross over Adrian's head.

'Come out, Satan!' Anna said.

And Mother said, 'Lord, banish the Devil from this my dear, dear son,' and she was weeping.

Then Rolandson said his piece again, and Anna and Mother, and they all went round and round one after the other very fast until they were simply chanting 'Out, Satan, out; out,

Satan, out!', as if they were at a football match; and now Maggie had joined in too with her bright intense face, leaning all her heavy weight on his leg, 'Out, Satan, out!'

Through all this while Adrian lay still as stone between them. But finally when they were exhausted and there was a moment's silence, he said, 'Finished? Finished?' and his voice was trembling and broken as he fished for his old sarcasm. 'Because I'm getting bored.'

Then Rolandson slapped him about the face and it all began again.

Shivering outside, I let all this happen; I let it happen and I prayed on and on to whoever it was I was praying to, I prayed, 'Don't let this happen, don't! Don't let them change him.' But it went on. Until at last I began to realize now what I should have realized all along, that if they changed Adrian, if he became one of them, I would have to change too. I would. Because I couldn't resist them on my own. And I realized that it was because of Adrian, because of his example and his courage and how I loved and at the same time hated him, that I was able to take the position I did, my neutral position in the family, in the middle, or rather aside, and just waiting quietly for the day I could leave all this and be myself. So my own fate really hung on his, hung on what it would mean if Adrian was able to be changed and broken. Because then they would change me.

I turned back to the window, shivering and hugging myself, and I watched silently. They were still chanting on, round and round. I should interrupt somehow, I thought. I should, I must *do* something, something that would sway that ugly battle. I mustn't simply be a spectator, because it was my battle too. Obviously it was. But I couldn't do anything. I was paralysed again. Because I had never never never taken a decisive part in anything, or shown my real self to anyone. I was the lukewarm one, cast out into outer darkness, gnashing my teeth in the rain here and peeping in through a crack in the curtains.

★   ★   ★

They were still holding him down and chanting when my father came in. It was typical of Father, I suppose, that he couldn't bear to spend even a single night in a different bed from my mother, and so he had come all the way back from London on the train and even gone to the extravagance of a taxi from Oxted, so as to be able to surprise her rather than phoning. He had a bunch of daffodils in his hands.

'Heavens,' he said. 'What on earth's going on here? The lad's not ill, is he?'

I heaved a great sigh of relief then because I thought, I thought, now my dear father was here, surely he wouldn't let this go on, because it wasn't his style; and I almost slunk away in the dark.

'He is possessed!' Rolandson said. He looked up at my father with fiery eyes full of challenge.

'He was organizing orgies with Maggie and Anne-Marie and lots of others, right here,' Anna said. 'In the woodshed.'

'It's our fault,' Mother said with a numb, dull voice. 'We weren't hard enough on him, dear, we never used our gifts.'

Adrian said sharply, 'Let me out of here, shit!'

Father was dazed. 'Orgies?' he said. 'How do you know?'

For the first time in the whole affair in the counselling room Maggie chipped in for herself.

'He made us have orgies together! He made us. Men are pigs.'

'Liar,' Adrian said. 'What crap! You're ill, love, that's what you are.'

'He *made* us!' she insisted, her cockney voice was shrill and edged with hysteria. 'He made us take all our clothes off in the woodshed and copulate together.'

Father said, in a faltering parody of his usual sternness, 'Is this true, Adrian? Tell me at once.' He looked confused and only now had he seen the broken plates on the floor. Rolandson's red eyes still fixed him.

Adrian said, 'If these people will let me go, I'll tell you.'

My father looked at Rolandson and Rolandson said distinctly, 'I'm afraid he was really violent, vicar. We can't let him go. You can see how much damage he's done already, he's possessed.'

'Oh balls!'

'I wish you'd watch your language,' my sister said.

'He *made* us!'

'Tell me the truth, Adrian.'

'Shit, can't you see, can't you see all of you? The girl's just jealous because she couldn't get Anne-Marie into her bed. She's a lesbian and not quite right in the head, we all knew that all along. I bet it was even her put those knickers in the wash on purpose. She's a loony and she's got the hots for . . .'

'Liar!' Maggie shouted.

'Satan is wily,' Rolandson said grimly.

And then my mother said timidly, 'I'm afraid he smashed all the plates in the cupboard, dear.'

My father looked lost. He stood there with the daffodils still in his hands, his black-brimmed hat on and rain on his glasses. And he must have realized now how difficult, how impossible it would be simply to end it all here and now, to send Adrian off to bed in a triumph that would make him quite untouchable. He stood there wavering, uncertain, and my mother said quietly, 'Remember the prophecy, dear. The Devil is in our midst and we must use our gifts.'

Silence.

Father took his hat off and pushed a hand into thick hair. Then he said half-heartedly, 'Let us pray,' and they all bowed their heads, except Adrian of course, who was still after all this time unbelievably pinned to the table; and my father prayed a short prayer for guidance.

Then silence again.

'Oh yawn,' Adrian said. 'Will you let me go to bed now? You'll never break me you know. Which is all you want to do in the end.'

Outside I was really beginning to shiver and shiver with the cold and the wet, and again I thought perhaps it was safe now and I could go. Adrian was so strong and surely Father wouldn't let Rolandson hit him again. Or perhaps I should just hurl a stone in through the window and that would end it? But then I thought no, they would probably just take that as an indication of the Devil's presence or something. There was no telling. Once you had God and the Devil there was just no telling what people would do.

'You'll never break me,' he said again, malicious, almost enjoying his strength.

Which angered my father. 'You keep silence, laddie,' he said, 'while we wait upon the Word of the Lord.'

'Yawn,' Adrian said, provocative. And suddenly I was angry too. Why did he have to be provocative? Why? Why shame them and hurt them and harm them and make everything more difficult? I was furious. They could never retreat if he went on like that. Why didn't he say, 'Look, honestly Dad, I'm not possessed. Why don't we just sit down together and talk it over reasonably?' But Adrian would never do that. He had to provoke. He had to win and humiliate. He didn't want reconciliation. And I thought again, perhaps he *was* possessed, and perhaps the Devil *was* in him. Who was to say the ins and outs of these things, why one person is provocative and another gentle? Perhaps he was possessed and deserved every bit of what he was getting.

But then if he was possessed, I thought, so was I in a way. So was I, with some of the things I thought and did and couldn't help doing. Perhaps we all were. Those three words came back to my mind, 'Ravishnah, homorrah homorrah!' and this time I let them come to my lips. I said them out loud for the first time, there in the pouring rain. 'Ravishnah, homorrah homorrah!', and I weighed them up. Sacred or profane? But nothing. Absolutely nothing. I was none the wiser.

'The Word of the Lord, eh?' Adrian pressed on, taunting. 'Looks like we could be here for the duration then. Couldn't be so kind as to get me a pillow, could you?'

But Rolandson began to speak in tongues, loud and fast and fluent; and this time there was something strong and extraordinarily persuasive about it, as if it really was a language and he was trying to persuade somebody of something, trying and trying, urging, struggling with some painful expression. He began suddenly, then his voice rose and rose. He took a hand away from Adrian's shoulder, persuading and thunderously persuading in this strange language – and Adrian didn't move.

He didn't move. And when Rolandson finished there was a long dark silence with every face tense in the dim yellow of the room, the headmaster on the wall dour there with his full glass of sherry. Adrian didn't struggle. Then:

'This is the Word of the Lord,' Rolandson said. He said it with surprising, almost shocking gentleness after what had gone before, and his face changed, relaxed, wore the same beatific smile it had had that first day he spoke in tongues in the pulpit a year ago. 'This is the Word of the Lord, and it is for you, Adrian, for *you*. For the Lord loves you intensely in spite of all, in spite of your mockery and blaspheming and lust. This is the Word of the Lord: My son, you are twisted and crippled by the Devil within you. You are twisted and crippled and warped within and without. And your foot and your lameness are just an outward sign of this. You have never run or jumped or played like others do. This is the outward sign of Satan, of his crippling power. But you are equally crippled within; you have never prayed, nor given, nor loved, not as others love, for Lucifer has twisted your soul. And tonight the Lord says to you, He says, Adrian, my son, I can make you *whole*, I and I only, Jahweh! I can heal your soul. I can cast out the Devil within you. I can give you prayer and happiness and real love. And I can heal your *body* too, your broken broken body; I can straighten that which the Devil has twisted so horribly and I can give you running and jumping and the play and exuberance of others.'

Adrian had begun to cry.

'And the only thing that prevents me from doing this miracle is your will. For you have a strong and manly will and I shall not violate it as Satan has. So I say to you now, I say, submit yourself to me. Submit yourself to me and all things shall be possible.'

If my father had had doubts before, he had surely lost them now. For who had ever brought Adrian to tears before? And Rolandson's voice was so strong, but kind, so rich and convincing and mysterious. Father put down the daffodils and his hat and layed his hands over Rolandson's on Adrian's forehead. And they all began to pray together in tongues again with people interrupting to say, 'Lucifer, the Lord *commands* thee to leave this boy!' and 'Lord, make Thy servant whole! Straighten that which the Devil has twisted!'

And Adrian wept.

Then they left off holding him down on the table because they saw he didn't struggle any more, he was still, and they knelt beside him and kept praying and shouting like that.

'Lucifer, in the Name of the Most High, thou art *banished* from the twisted body of this boy!'

And Adrian wept and finally he shouted – he shouted half-strangled, 'Help me, help me, Lord.'

*   *   *

They all burst out singing different songs together. They cracked their voices singing for joy and Maggie was all but delirious. Adrian had cried for help. He had called upon the Name of the Lord. They clapped their hands together, singing and singing.

Then I couldn't bear it any longer. I couldn't. It was as if I was taken, suddenly filled and swept with rage, like those swine who plunged from the cliff. Because they were going to change Adrian; they were going to break him and change him. Utterly. And then they would change me. Because they wouldn't rest there, with him. They would never rest from changing people with all their tongues and prophecies and words of wisdom. They would change me and everybody, transform everybody into themselves, until the whole world was ay-mening and praising the Lord and casting out demons and we were all and always, constantly, swept with emotion and suffocated with guilt.

And anyway, they had tricked Adrian with his foot, hadn't they? It wasn't a real conversion. They would never have beaten him without his foot. It was a dirty, filthy trick

129

to make my brother weep like that, who had never wept before.

So when he didn't struggle anymore but cried through his tears, 'Help me, help me, Lord Jesus!' – I was taken and filled with rage. I ran. It was like a delirious happiness of fury and action I was taken with. I ran to the front door and along the long corridors to the kitchen, my heels echoing, head pounding with blood. Ran and ran. And it was so natural then, what I did. It was like I had always had the plan in my head. Natural as an animal, wounded, exhausted, twisting in self-preservation.

In the huge kitchen next to the counselling room, I turned on the gas oven, opened the door, but I didn't light it. I stood a second, shivering and trembling together, twisting around to weigh up that room. And then I opened the tap on the great paraffin drum they used to feed all the heaters in the place. I screwed open the tap and the stuff splashed out dark and blue on to bare floorboards. It seemed to take an age, dripping and splashing and inching its way across the floorboards. I ran to the door and looked up and down the corridor. No one. They were all in bed. There was only the sound of the others singing and chanting still in the next room, changing him. But nobody else. So there was still time, I told myself, still time to stop. But I didn't even hesitate. They were changing him, breaking him in there, and every moment was a part of him that was changed and lost, and a part of me they would be able to change later. I ran to the windows and smashed them. You needed air for a fire, didn't you? You needed air. But nobody must know they'd been opened on purpose. So smash them. The gas was beginning to smell. The puddle of paraffin fanned across the floor. Now! The matches. Damn, where were the matches? For a moment I couldn't find them. The gas hissed.

I ran all over the kitchen looking for the matches, jumping over and over the patch of paraffin. The voices in the next room were louder and louder, rising to a crescendo. Was Adrian's amongst them? Was he changed already? Where were the matches? Damn! And I prayed, 'Help me, help me dear God to find the matches. Help me! Don't let them change him.' In the drawer beside the cooker of course. Were they? Yes. Yes yes yes, a huge box of Brymay. Now then? I went to the door, fumbling with five or six matches all together, lit them in a great flare, burning my fingertips, and tossed them over my head into the hissing and gurgling behind. And I ran.

It was like a sudden wild blast of wind in an empty silent place, the bursting of those flames in that room. I ran. I didn't turn to look but I felt the sudden draft like a long shiver through the bones of this stale school. 'Fire, fire!' I dashed down the corridor screaming, 'Fire!' and I burst into the counselling room.

'Fire! Fire! In the kitchen. There's a fire!'

They were all still knelt and singing softly 'Raised on a Dove's Wings', and Adrian whimpering on the table.

'It's burning down. Fire! We've got to get everybody out of their beds. They'll be killed!'

From the kitchen already there was a fierce sound of crackling and smashing and then a muffled explosion full of breakages. And as they struggled to their feet, their spell likewise was exploded and broken and shattered: I grabbed Adrian's arm, heaved him off the table and out toward the connecting door with the assembly hall. We slithered over broken china, him almost a dead weight and everybody around scurrying and shouting. Then I saw Mother's hand-bag was there on a chair by the door and I picked it up automatically, as if I had known all along what I must do, controlled and guided as I was by this fury. I picked up the bag and shoved Adrian through the assembly hall, through the french windows and out on to the terrace.

'Fire! Fire in the kitchen! Call the fire-brigade!'

Adrian stood dazed, weeping on the terrace in the rain, hanging on to my shoulder.

'Ricky, Ricky, what's happening?'

I rummaged through the bag, smelt the same old smell of Mother's bag, tissues and worn-out gloves, found the purse, found some notes inside, I couldn't see what denomination, and stuffed them into his jeans' pocket. He had lost his coat somewhere. I said, 'Run!'

'Ricky,' he wept. He wept and wept. 'What's happening? What are they doing to me?'

I couldn't say anything. I felt the rage beginning to go and I was scared. I was scared by him weeping, I didn't want him to weep, and was scared by the fire. I was scared by the people sleeping in their beds. I shivered, soaked to the bone.

'What did they do to me? Ricky, the power in that room. I couldn't believe it. The power. They might have done it. Who knows? Perhaps they might have.' You could scarcely make out what he was saying, his voice was so broken with emotion and garbled. 'The power there, Ricky. You couldn't, you couldn't resist it.'

The rain swept against us and there was a growing light now began to dance and flicker on the sward as flames twisted upward, leaping and flapping from the kitchen windows.

'Take the money,' I said. 'Take the money. Go to London. You've got friends. Go to London. Don't talk to them here again. They only want to break you.'

But he wasn't listening. He was suddenly bent down, pulling up the bell-bottoms of his jeans to see his foot.

'The power,' he muttered. 'Who knows?' But then he

sighed. In the spreading glow of flames through the rain you could see his foot there the same as ever, skew and twisted.

'They tricked you with that,' I said.

He stood up. He wiped his face on his sleeve and his features settled a little now. He pushed his chin out with the little goaty beard.

'They tricked you with your foot,' I said. 'I watched in at the window.'

He turned sharply to look at me. Our faces were wet with rain and tears both and his eyes took a sudden light from the flames beyond, not so much a colour as a depth of reflection, a glow almost, like the day he'd watched me over the dinner table when Father prayed. A glow of coals.

'They tricked you,' I said. And I began to feel desperate again. I don't know why. But desperate and guilty. His eyes went right into me.

'They tricked you. You don't think they could have really done it, do you?'

He stared at me, his long hair plastered into his face and neck.

'They couldn't really have healed you.'

Then he looked away. He shrugged his shoulders. 'So why didn't you come sooner, Ricky? You should have come sooner.'

And after another moment he muttered, 'Sooner, or not at all. But not then.'

We watched each other again another minute and he was still crying, but silently now, out of glowing eyes. The fire ran beyond us, a quick liquid orange shooting up the walls of the place against the night behind. And he shouted:

'You were watching, my God? Why didn't you come sooner?'

'When he hit me? Why didn't you come?'

I couldn't speak.

'You secretive secretive little bastard,' he said. 'You bastard!' and he turned then and stumbled off with the rolling crippled half run he had, across the deep mud and down to the pine woods.

Behind me in the school a bell had begun to ring fierce and shrill and everybody was shouting. I turned, and the fire racing up that wall, hissing and spitting and crackling, it seemed to me now it was spitting out those three awful words, 'Ravishnah, homorrah homorrah' – hissing and shouting them in sparks and tongues of flame – 'Ravishnah, homorrah homorrah!' – shouting them for the very last time it must be from the hell of that boiling fire – and I was sick.

★   ★   ★

So Copplesford was burnt down, but nobody was hurt, excepting a girl who broke her leg, jumping unnecessarily out of a window. It took the fire-brigade the best part of an hour to find their way there through the wet country roads and with all the wooden floors it had the place was already lost. So the next year's houseparty was held at Mickleham instead about ten miles away.

The police said it was the result of somebody carelessly leaving the gas on, and then an explosion. They didn't look into it too carefully, I don't suppose. There was no reason to. My father instead and Rolandson too, they said it was the work of the Devil, of Satan in our midst. But they said it really a bit half-heartedly, and it seemed somehow the Sword of the Spirit had been blunted and broken and burnt out of them by that fire.

Adrian didn't come home – we didn't hear from him at all – and my father took it badly and bitterly, pacing the floor of his study, shredding oranges with his fingernails and shouting 'No, no!' to himself out loud when the rest of the house was quiet and silent at night. 'No, no no!' he shouted. He paced his room, clutching sticky fingers in his hair. And now he said it had been a grave mistake to try to exorcize Adrian against his will and that Rolandson had had no right to initiate such a thing in his, my father's absence, and that my mother had been incredibly, unutterably foolish to go along with him like that – and on nothing more than the indictment of a stupid trollop like Maggie! It was stupefying! He began to fall out with Rolandson on every possible occasion until finally the curate asked to leave before the end of his three-year period and my father said, 'Willingly.' My mother kept silent and accepted all criticism. She said it was all her fault and she must bear the responsibility, and Anna said precisely what Father said about it and about everything else as well and she broke off trying to get Rolandson to marry her.

Maggie went too. She disappeared a week or so after the fire. She didn't say a word. My mother tried to find her by phoning everybody she knew. She phoned the Metropolitan Police Training Centre where she worked but they said Maggie wasn't there any more. They said she had been discharged three months ago for obscene behaviour and inciting others to mischief. My mother didn't tell us this but I heard her say it to my father when they left the kitchen door open once and I was outside. You always heard everything sooner or later if you wanted to. But where Maggie had set off to so brightly every morning those past three months remained an absolute mystery. Unless it was to meet the girl she called 'lovey' at the Hen and Chickens wine bar in Crouch End.

*　　　*　　　*

They stopped speaking out loud in tongues in church. It seemed simply they'd lost the gusto for it. It was back to 1666. My father put the manuscript of his book in the cubby hole under the stairs with all his old sermon notes and he said he would finish it when he had a bit more energy. He didn't seem to have an awful lot of energy these days, he said, and he complained about being short of breath when he went up the stairs.

'I wonder where Adrian is?' he said at dinner – and he didn't air his views at the table any more because there was no one to argue with. He seemed to have lost all interest and confidence. 'I used to like having a good discussion with Adrian,' he said vaguely. Then my mother had to turn away sharply, showing how her hair behind was completely grey. She rummaged furiously in the larder and I got up quick too and took the dog out. I took the dog out and round the back I fed the last rabbit, because there was still one last rabbit hanging on. But it would die soon I thought. Or perhaps I would go to the polytechnic first and it would cease to be my responsibility. My mother would have to look after it until it died. It didn't bother me any more. Then when I thought she would have dried her eyes I went back in again.

Anna became a lady-worker and so when Rolandson went back to South Africa she helped my father and he didn't have another curate because the bishop thought the church was going to be hard-pressed in the seventies and they would have to make savings. She drove him round to meetings and to visit the sick in her car because he couldn't drive because of his eyesight: he had no energy these days, he said; he couldn't use his bicycle at all. She sang in old people's homes at Christmas-time and organized the carol service. I went to the polytechnic to study physics and Mother took paying lodgers into the house who had nothing to do with the church, and she said, 'Bless their dear souls,' in a sad kind of way when they broke something in their rooms or when they left without paying the last month's rent.

Then it was 1973 Father fell ill and they discovered he had cancer and it was quite advanced. He was going to die. My mother was almost destroyed with sorrow and my sister likewise, incredulous at the very idea of his death, as he himself for so long was quite incredulous. But while he was dying nobody came to heal him or lay hands on him, and nobody spoke in tongues with him over his drugged and suffering body – for he died in some pain. Neither my mother nor Anna spoke in tongues. But only at the very last Adrian came, and he had short smart hair and a plain-looking pleasant wife we had never seen before. He was clean-shaven and he worked for an advertising agency and you could never have imagined he had ever been possessed by a demon. He sat with Father and held his hand, helped him to the commode and back, and he quickly made peace with my mother and Anna so that after the funeral we all laughed together a moment in the lounge recalling Father when he used to say 'Stupefying!' and eat so many oranges.

But to me on his own before he left, Adrian said, 'You always were a secretive little bastard, Ricky, a sneaky sod.' That was what he said to me before he left. So that looking back now, looking back at that long year when the Sword of the Spirit came to our house and the dove and tongues of flame, I am never sure really whether the Devil was in him, or in me, or in Maggie perhaps, or even in Rolandson – only that a devil there must have been somewhere, the way our family had sheared apart and crumbled, like a house built on sand.